The Boss

Sheena Tempest

Contents

Prologue

Maybe I'm scared,because you mean more to me than any other person.

You areeverything I think about,everything I need,everything I want.

+++

The day at work went by as usual until Mr. Connor requested for all his schedules today to be cleared and needed me in his office in five minutes.

Weird. He don't usually do that unless it was something urgent. Surely, there must be something wrong.

Rushing to his office, I curled my fingers around the cooling metal as I opened the handle. Taking in a deep breathe, I prayed that it wasn't something bad as I entered his office.

He was standing by the window as his back faced me. My eyes took noticed of the usual features of his muscled arm covered by his sleeves and the toned six packs underneath his dress shirt.

But, the relationship between us were purely just boss and secretary. Nothing more, nothing less.

He turned around, my eyes travelling down his high cheekbones to his chiseled jaws. A waft of aftershave hit my nostrils as I assumed that he had just shaved his stubbles.

His dark hooded eyes looked into mine as it raked across my body. That was something that I would catch him doing when I was in his office.

I didn't take it to heart, purely thinking that he must be satisfied with the attire I wore for work. Since I was his personal assistant, it was a rule to be nicely dressed.

But this time, the look in his eyes were different. His eyes were clouded with lust and desire.

I cleared my throat as I wetted my chapped lips. "Do you have any instructions for me, sir?" I asked, closing the door behind me.

"Come here, Natalie." He motioned for me to move towards him with a flick of his hand.

I did as I was told and moved towards him until I was right beside his desk. My eyes glanced down at the polished desk, nothing on it. It was even spotless.

I looked up to see him gone until I was pushed to the back as I leaned against the desk. His arms trapped me by my sides as I swallowed my saliva.

"Mr. Connor..." I trailed off, taking in the breath-taking view of him. My eyes examined the close-up of his face which I hadn't had a chance to, as I inwardly sighed.

My eyes lingered on his beautiful lips just as I felt his fingers travelling down my thighs.

I gasped when they lingered on my inner thighs. I felt my undies dripping wet at the effect he had on me.

Darn it, I was feeling like a complete slut.

When they were about to go further, I closed my eyes and waited for the moment to come.

It never did as I opened my eyes to see his lips curled into a smirk. Leaning in, his lips brushed past my ear. "You like that, didn't you?" His voice was dangerously low as his lips left feathery kisses down my neck.

I moaned his name when his lips lingered on my sensitive spot, my hands clamped against the desk behind me for support.

His fingers tilted my jaws to face him. "Tell me you want me, tell me you need me." He whispered, looking into my glazed eyes as I found myself in a dilemma.

I want it so bad, not because I was horny right now. I had wanted it right from the start.

But, I didn't know that this was what he wanted as well. What should I do?

+++

1: I want it, but I can't

I felt my breath hitched at the back of my throat as I stared at him, pausing to breathe when I was stunned by the gorgeous creature in front of me.

He dipped his head into the crook of my neck as his nose tenderly brushed across my sensitive spot. I clenched my fists tightly as I held back a moan.

"I want it so badly right from the start, Mr. Connor." I whispered as his face hovered in front of me, his eyes staring at my lips. His hand reached out for my face but I grabbed it, even before he could hold my face.

"But I know that I can't." I blinked a couple of times as I slid past his body and dashed out of his office.

When I was sure that he had not followed after me, I wiped off the sweat that had trickled down my forehead as I sat back down on my desk.

My heart beat rapidly as I found my forehead leaning against my desk. I was in a state of dilemma. I didn't know what I really wanted.

But, would he fire me for rejecting him on the spot? I mean which boss wouldn't if his secretary rejected him when all he wanted was sex.

I must be crazy to think that my boss would have feelings for me. He was the director of the company and heck, maybe the sexiest boss in history.

He would definitely not spare me another glance if I didn't have what he wanted. All he wanted was just a good f*ck. But the thought of having sex again hit me.

I had lost my virginity at the age of 21 when I was drinking in a nightclub. That was the first and the last sex I had before I met Mr. Connor.

He was the gorgeous man who ruled the company in his own way ever since he was 20 and he had not once spared me a glance before. So why would he even look at me differently now?

Shame on me that I had actually craved for his attention and for his hands to be all over me. I was just like any other women who wanted his d*ck to slide into my womanhood.

What was I doing with my life?

A beep from my phone made me tilted up my head as I stared at the message. I was summoned to the underground as there would be a match between the boxer I attended to, Pitbull and another rising star, Brawn.

However, it seemed like Pitbull was going to retire soon and hand his 'champion' title over to his nephew, Viper who would be upholding his name as he takes over his uncle in boxing.

And according to him, I would be required to switch my loyalty to his nephew as I attend to him whenever he was badly injured. I was required to be professional at all times since this was an illegal match in the underground and if he was sent to the hospital, it would attract attention from the cops.

I had been attending to Pitbull for nearly five years, so I knew how it was done.

I just hope that his nephew would not give me trouble since I was informed that he was just a few years older than me.

I don't need his nephew to screw me while I had to stay by his side as his private medic.

My eyes lingered on the clock hands until it struck exactly five. Pulling on my bomber jacket, I grabbed my helmet and my bag as I rushed down to the lobby.

I had to be there by six, so I had to get there fast. And the only option was to drive there directly without caring if I was still in my office attire.

Tugging down my hair tie, I secured the straps of my helmet as I started the ignition. Getting onto my motorbike, I began to drive out of the parking lot.

2: Viper is Boss?

I continued to ride under the lamplight as I waited for the traffic light to turn orange before I sped across the road, not caring if it had turned red. I couldn't afford to waste my time stuck in the traffic.

My motorbike sped down the dark alley as I rounded the corner. The path led to the basement as I drove down the lane. It was as if I had done it several times. The dark didn't scare me at all.

When I reached, I got off from my motorbike and hurriedly brisk-walked to the door where a man was guarding it. He smiled at me when he recognised me and let me enter.

I walked into the arena where the fight has started. Ignoring the lustful stares from the male audiences, I tucked out my button-up blouse as I headed to the room.

When I reached Pitbull's room, I found the fifty year old wrapping his fists with bandages as he move to tighten the ends. When he had trouble securing the ends, I moved forward and helped him.

He shot me a lopsided smile as he released a sigh. "You have been with me for five years, Natalie." He chuckled deeply, cocking his head to one side as he smiled down at me.

I nodded, smiling along with him. "Yes, sir." I said, not looking up as I secured the bandage wrapped around his left fist.

"By the way, I have someone to introduce to you." He said, motioning for the person to come out of the shadows.

When the light hit his face, I found myself gasping in shock. "Boss." I murmured, covering my mouth with my hands.

"Natalie." He smirked down at me while I turned to look at Pitbull who looked surprised as well.

"Ahh, seems like both of you know each other." He chuckled, shaking his head. I gulped as I turned to look at Boss who was wearing a wife beater and jeans with a leather jacket.

He looked so hot when he wasn't in his usual suit.

"Like what you see?" He smirked, making me look down in embarrassment. What was I thinking? He was just fooling around with me.

"Natalie may be your private medic, but she is off limits, boy." Pitbull said, smacking his shoulder. He nodded with a smile on his face. "I will try to, uncle."

He stood up and shook his head. "You and your playboy ways should really change, Declan." And with that, he left the room as he went off for his fight.

I looked around the surroundings to find that we were alone. Would he do anything to me? I mean, we were now no longer boss and secretary. He might use this chance to get back at me for rejecting him, wouldn't he?

I moved to sit down on the bench when he wasn't talking as he just stared at me. I held onto my helmet tightly as I looked at the ground as though it was the most interesting thing on Earth.

I felt the bench creaked as he sat down beside me. Before I knew it, I was pulled to his laps as I gasped in shock. I tried to pull away from his arms, but he just wouldn't budge.

His fingers caressed my face while I struggled under his iron grip. "Stop struggling." He growled before his lips attacked mine.

My eyes widened as I stared at his face. Before long, I felt my eyelids closed as I tugged onto his wife beater and deepened the kiss.

His tongue slipped into my mouth as our lips moved in sync. He bit on my bottom lip until it was swollen. He pulled away and trailed kisses along my neck.

I moaned when he bit on my sensitive spot and left hickeys behind. I was pulled back to my senses as I quickly opened my eyes and pushed him away. Turning around, my fingers fumbled with my collar as I adjusted it.

"We really shouldn't be doing this, boss." I mumbled as I pulled down the hems of my skirt. I was pulled back to his arms as he stared down at me.

I felt myself looking back into his dark hooded eyes as he let out a possessive growl.

"You are mine, Natalie Marsh."

+++

Vote. Comment. Share

Enjoying this book? Add this book to your library and your reading list.

Things are going to get interesting soon, you know? So, stay tuned for more.

4th July 2016

3: Against Him

"Absurd." I croaked out, feeling my core dripping wet as the stare manipulated my thoughts.

I imagined his fingers working skillfully through my whole body, giving me the pleasure which rocked my core.

I was really turning into a pathetic slut. The desire and lust for him was growing stronger that I had to rest my hands against his hard chest as I took in a deep breath.

With all my might, I pushed him off my body, tearing away the space which enclosed us.

I feared that I might let him have his way if I didn't do something to stop my wild imagination.

I looked up, giving him a pained look as I shook my head vigorously. "I can't do this." I let the words slipped out of my mouth as I turned around to escape.

He let me go. But I knew that it wouldn't be long before he caught me again.

Clutching onto my helmet tightly, I darted my way out of the crowd as I tightened my bomber jacket close to my skin, feeling the sensation relishing me again when I imagined him touching me.

Shaking off all the thoughts, I mentally slapped myself as I got out of the arena unnoticed.

Without even bidding the man goodbye like I usually did, I ignored his curious glance and sped out of the dark alley.

I kept my eyes trained on the road as images of the kiss filled my mind. I was going to go berserk soon if those dirty thoughts doesn't go away.

Ugh, what was wrong with me? He was just fooling around with me.

Declan.

His name sent a shiver down my spine as I felt my breath hitched at the back of my throat.

I shook my head and cleared my mind as I pulled up by the driveway. I fished into my pockets before letting my fingers travelled to my arms when it dawned on me that I had forgotten my bag.

I was in dipsh*t this time.

I fished into my pockets for my phone as I called boss. The call went straight to his voicemail while I dragged my face down in distraught.

Sure, I was in dipsh*t this time. I hopped onto my motorbike and drove back to the road.

+++

I woke up, my hair in a heap of mess as I stretched my limbs. I had slept on my working desk the entire night since the building was still open, even though it was late when I reached.

Thankfully, the guard let me through and allowed me to stay for a night.

If not, I would have to sleep on the streets.

A 'thud' on my desk made me looked up to see boss standing in front of me in his usual suit. It was so different from the dress code last night.

It made me almost couldn't recognised him if not for the pair of dark hooded eyes.

I eyed my bag on my desk and looked back up to see a smirk tugged on the end of his lips.

How I wish I could wipe that smirk off his face. It was because of him that had made me homeless for a night.

I was so going to get back at him for what he had done to me.

"You're angry." He simply said, folding his arms as he watched me flattened down my hair.

"Am I?" I calmly said, hiding my anger as the words came out smoothly.

"Your eyes gave away your emotions. Just like how you gave off the desire and lust which sparked in your eyes last night." His words earned a non-chalant shrug from me.

Well, two can play that game.

"You're right." You're wrong. I said, standing up from my desk.

"You're good at this." You're lousy at this. I said, slowly walking towards him. With each step I took, I tried not to let my confidence wavered at his condescending smirk.

"But you can't deny that you don't feel the same way as well." Because you did feel the lust and desire for me. I smirked, resting a hand on his shoulder while the other hand travelled down to his tie, gently tugging on it.

"Sorry, boss. But I won't let you have what you want, Declan." I finished, letting his name rolled out of my tongue oh so perfectly as I straightened his crooked tie.

Taking a step back, I grabbed my bag from the desk as I turned on my heels.

I felt fingers curled around my wrist as tingles shot through my arm. I ignored how the calmness overwhelmed me when he touched me.

It meant nothing.

I turned around to see a smirk tugged on his lips. "Where do you think you are going while you are in this state? Follow me." He said, his mask hiding all emotions as he jerked his head to the direction of his office.

I have a bad feeling that following him into his office would not turn out good.

+++

Vote. Comment. Share

Enjoying this book? Add this book to your library and your reading list.

Things are going to get interesting soon, you know? So, stay tuned for more.

11th July 2016

4: The Game Has Yet To Start

I followed behind him, trying my hardest to pull down my blouse from the unglam creases. When I reached his office, the familiar enclosed walls overwhelmed me as I took in calming deep breaths.

I will not let him have his way with me whether it's in the present or the future.

I watched as he entered through a door while I stared into space. What was that? A secret room? Oh god, was there where he held women captive and had fun with them?

"Are you coming in or what?" His voice rang through the room before silence engulfed the whole office. I gulped, moving my feet as they moved towards his room.

I stood by the doorway and stared at the sight. Everything was ordinary, nothing fanciful or obscene. I heaved a sigh of relief and entered the room when a shopping bag was hung in front of me.

I looked up with a raised brow, puzzled that he would have a shopping bag here.

"Don't worry," He paused, his breath fanning my neck as he took a step closer. I stared at him, both feet rooted to the ground as his lips curved into a smirk. "It's an office attire that I had bought for you beforehand."

"I knew that this was going to happen." He shrugged, slipping the shopping bag into my hands.

"You seem to have foreseen this, huh?" I said, letting my fingers dig into the shopping bag. I pulled the outfit out and smiled in contentment.

He didn't seem to have a bad taste either.

"Seems like I have bought the right outfit." He whispered, closing the distance between us as his eyes scanned my face.

I forced a shrug, biting my bottom lips to control my crazy hormones which was running all over the place right now.

His smirk faltered as a cold façade took over his handsome face. He tilted his head to the side, his eyes rested on something. "There's a bathroom here for you to use." He said, turning his head back to me as he looked at me once more before walking past me.

I released a breath which I didn't know I had been holding and quickly rushed into the bathroom.

+++

I quickly keyed in my password as I checked through any new emails in my inbox. I read all of them, mostly unimportant ones before moving on to check boss's schedules.

He was going to have a conference meeting at 12 noon today. This meant that I would have to skip lunch again.

I sighed, picking up a small stack of files which were meant for him to sign. Pulling down the ends of my pencil skirt, I inwardly groaned in frustration.

He had purposely bought a smaller size which made my ass almost noticeable. He deliberately did that just to check out my ass.

Well, two can play that game.

I slowly made my way towards his office as I knocked on the door. "Come in." He replied from inside. I quickly pushed past the door and stepped into his office.

His head tilted up from the stack of papers on his desk as he smirked at me. Each step I walked towards him, I would always have the urge to pull it down.

But I did not. I was going to make fun of him for as long as I can.

I placed the files in front of him while his eyes continued to scan the rest of my body. I badly wanted to roll my eyes at him and show him the PMS side of me.

"Boss, these are the files requested to be signed," I paused, ignoring how his eyes twinkled with mischief as though he was imagining something naughty that involved me.

"And for the conference later at 12, do you have any other materials that you need? I will send them for printing before the conference starts." I finished, swallowing my saliva as I waited for any further instructions.

It was killing me that I was trying my best not to give in to my desires.

I watched as he fiddled with his chin, thinking. "I only need the contracts. I suppose they are already prepared beforehand, aren't they?" He confirmed with that knowing look on his face.

I simply nodded in reply. "Good. Remember, your presence is needed, whether you like it or not." He said the last part so lowly that I shivered at his words.

"You are dismissed." He said, flicking me off with a wave of his hand. I turned on my heels and curved my lips into a smirk.

As I walked out of his office, I deliberately swayed my hips to add effect to my barely covered ass thanks to his short pencil skirt.

I could feel holes burning behind me, probably attracting his attention. Who said that he was the only one who could tease me?

I could do the same as well.

+++

Vote. Comment. Share

Enjoying this book? Add this book to your library and your reading list.

19th July 2016

5: Tiny Bit Of Affection

I held onto the clipboard with the contracts needed for the conference in one minute time.

My flats kissed the polished floor as I followed after Mr. Connor who was taking large strides towards the direction of the conference room.

Before he entered, he whipped his head in my direction and raked his eyes over my body.

Though disgusted under his gaze, I looked at him in the eye confidently.

He pulled me into his arms while I struggled under his grasps and furrowed my brows deeply.

"Boss---" I was cut off by his index finger as he dipped his head to the crook of my neck, his breath fanning my ear.

"Be careful later," He paused, closing his eyes. "The man I'm signing a contract with is a womanizer and he will do anything to get in your pants if he catches his eyes on you." His words made my breath hitch at the back of my throat.

I nodded solemnly, pulling my pencil skirt down as far as possible. The last thing I needed was to attract that man with my barely covered ass.

He nodded in satisfaction and let me go. Turning on his heels, he opened the door of the conference room and entered.

I followed after him and forced a smile as I was met with an older looking man who had unshaven stubbles. His eyes were planted firmly on his PA who was wearing a blood red bandeau bra and black pencil skirt.

Slut was the first word that popped into my mind. She was flirting with the man who was oblivious of our presence.

Boss cleared his throat as he stood on the other side of the long stretch of desk. I walked towards him and stood beside him as we watched the man buttoning up his shirt.

His eyes rested on Boss with a smile and shook hands with him. "It's a pleasure to meet you, Mr. Connor."

"Likewise, Mr. Anderson."

They sat down while we, PAs took our seats. His eyes flickered to me as his lips curved into a smirk while his eyes rested on my chest.

I looked towards his PA who was glaring at me. I inwardly groaned, disgusted with his gaze on my chest.

He was exactly like what Boss said, a womanizer and had dark motives.

"Mr. Anderson, about the contract, do you agree to our company's clauses? It was agreed in the previous meeting that each of our company will possess 50% of the shares in this project." He started while I sighed in relief when his attention was turned back to Boss.

His beautiful PA, on the other hand, was practically drooling over Boss. I wanted to dig out her eyes for even looking at him this way.

Wait, what the hell was wrong with me? I shouldn't be so jealous over this trivial matter. He wasn't even my property.

I buried my jealousy which popped out of nowhere and maintained my composure as the two CEOs discussed about their collaboration on this project.

Throughout the whole conversation, I noticed that Mr. Anderson was doing something that was tickling his PA.

Must be some PDA again.

His eyes met mine with his lips curving into a smirk. I shivered slightly under his burning gaze and looked down at the clipboard in my hands.

I felt a leg touching mine as I silently gasped in surprise. Looking under the desk, I noticed his leg caressing mine while I shivered in disgust.

This man had the audacity to touch me after touching his own PA.

I tilted my head up to be met with his eyes which held mischief in them.

Before I could respond, a leg swooped down in front of mine. I turned my head to see Boss trying to control himself while Mr. Anderson caressed his legs.

His gaze stayed on him the entire time as they discussed about the project.

My heart suddenly warmed at the sight. He was trying to protect me.

Who could have thought that the playboy in front of me who was always trying to f*ck me would actually help me?

Instinctively, I reached out for his hand as my fingers entwined with his, silently thanking him.

He held onto mine as though I was his lifeline while he tried to keep himself from showing his pained expression.

I closed my eyes for a bit before opening them to see the leg slowly reaching to crotch.

I can't allow his leg to reach it.

Without warning, I grasped onto his leg and snapped my head towards Mr. Anderson.

His eyes widened slightly at my actions before smirking at me.

I moved his leg until it touched the floor, clenching my jaws in anger.

I hated jerks like him.

After that, he didn't make any move on me but moved on to his beautiful PA instead.

I sighed in relief, watching as they signed the contracts and scanned through the clauses once more.

When both parties were satisfied, Mr. Anderson stood up and walked towards Boss as they shook hands.

His eyes then rested on mine as he winked at me. I gulped, staring at the front as I felt a hand groping my ass.

I jumped immediately at his action and looked towards him with a glare. An arm was draped around my waist as I was pulled towards Boss who held me in a protective manner.

"It has been a pleasure to meet you, but my PA is off limits to you, Derrick."
He said through gritted teeth as he stared at Mr. Anderson with a cold
glance.

He let his hand fall back to his side as he nodded in amusement. "Alright
then, Declan. I'm not going to touch her because I am giving you face." He
finished, before striding out of the office with his PA following after him
like a lost puppy.

I released a breath which I didn't know I had been holding before looking
towards Boss who was staring at me intently.

Immediately, I pulled away and let my eyes dropped to the floor as I rubbed
my nape in embarrassment.

+++

Vote. Comment. Share

Enjoying this book? Add this book to your library and your reading list.

I don't know if you guys prefer 1000+ words chapter but I had to make it
this long for the triggered scene ;) Hope you've enjoyed!

25th July 2016

6: A Promise To Make Me His

M y eyes shifted uncomfortably as his intense stare continued to stay on me.

"Boss." I cleared my throat, my grip on the clipboard tightened.

"You were jealous when his PA was drooling over me." He said, walking towards me while I backed away.

"I-I didn't." Denial.

His lips curled into a smirk. "Really? It's hard to believe that you didn't."

My eyebrows furrowed as I frowned upon his words.

In one moment I was standing. In the next, I was leaning against the desk as his arms trapped my sides.

"Boss---" He cut me off with his lips pressed against mine.

I closed my eyes and bit back a moan as his tongue skimmed across my lips.

His tongue dived into my mouth, our tongues dominating as I was lost in my own fantasy.

My fingers looped his belt as I pulled him closer and closer to me, closing every single gap which kept us apart.

His fingers slid down from my arms to my waist before it went down to my barely covered ass. My panties tightened as his touch sent shivers down to my core.

F*ck, he made me wet.

His tongue slowly withdrew from my mouth and pulled away, our noses barely touching.

I stared at him, my eyes filled with lust and desire as our hot pants filled the room.

He groped my ass and carried me to the desk. My barely covered ass kissed the cooling surface of the desk as I felt my breath hitched at the back of my throat.

His lips met mine hungrily as his fingers moved down to my inner thighs. He hooked his fingers into my panties, sliding a finger into my wet entrance.

"You are wet for me, only me." He purred seductively, pulling his finger out of my hole before pushing it in forcefully while my walls tightened and loosened at each jam of his finger.

"Mhm, not a virgin." He whispered, leaving feathery kisses along my neck.

I felt my fists tightened at his word, 'virgin'. Using all my mental strength, I pushed him away from me and adjusted my panties and skirt.

He gazed at me with a shock expression before his lips tilted up into a smirk.

"Interesting. You make me so curious every second that I want you so badly."

I frowned upon his words, glaring at him. "I am not a possession." I hissed through gritted teeth, biting my lips to stop myself from yelling at him.

It was after all still office hours and he was still my boss.

His arms were wrapped around my waist, pulling me towards him until our noses were touching. "You are not a possession. But you will become my woman soon."

It was a promise, a vow to make me as his woman. I gulped in panic.

"I'll do it at all costs, even if I have to seduce you." He purred seductively, his breath sending shivers down my spine.

His words were enough to make my core dripping wet.

What the f*ck? I won't let him have what he wants.

+++

I placed the freshly brewed coffee on his desk, handing him a few files for his approval.

His lips skimmed across the rim of the cup as his eyes raked over my body.

After that moment in the conference room, he made it a rule that only he could choose what I wore at work.

I f*cking hate this rule, but he was still my boss. I couldn't defy him, could I? My head would be the first to roll if I did.

He loved it when I wore incredibly short skirt and tight blouse, said that I should show off my curves often.

But during lunchtime, I would sneak off to the cafeteria with my bomber jacket to cover my revealing outfit.

Yeah right, show off my curves. More like showing him what he would be getting if he gets me in his bed.

Which would not be happening in his wildest dreams.

"Come here, Natalie." He waved me over while I stood next to him, staring at the files he was pointing at.

I felt a hand tug my wrist as I was pulled to his laps.

His fingers caressed my cheeks, his thumb brushing across my sensitive spot on my neck while I moaned without control.

"Your moans always drives me crazy." He whispered, his breath fanning my face as our noses barely touched.

"So sexy." He cooed, trailing kisses along my neck. His hands curled the back of my neck, shifting my head to the side for him to have more access.

His lips moved down to my blouse as he unbuttoned the first three buttons, leaving my black bra in full view.

His lips gently kissed the top of my bra, making my nipples hardened without real contact.

The game hasn't started and he has already taken the lead. Who said that I was going to let him do that?

+++

Vote. Comment. Share

Enjoying this book? Add this book to your library and your reading list.

1st August 2016

7: Strike

His lips continued to attack against my skin as I sealed my lips, biting back a moan.

I can't let him have the satisfaction of how his actions made me felt pleasure within.

"Boss..." I trailed off, feeling his fingers digging into my skin as his lips left feathery kisses along my shoulder.

"What is it? Tell me what you want." He purred seductively, moving his fingers to my last button before throwing my blouse across the desk.

I gasped at his action, feeling my skin being exposed to him with only my bra staying in place.

His fingers skimmed across my skin, slowly bidding his time as he tortured me with each second passed.

"Tell me, baby. Tell me what you want and I will give it to you." He purred again, gently and slowly sucking against my skin with his fingers moving to my back.

Tugging on my clasp, he teased me while nipping against my skin.

I felt my core aroused, feeling the need to have him inside of me.

Knowing that I was almost losing it, I clenched my fists and sealed my lips tightly.

My bottom lips gradually turned swollen with my attempts to hold back my desperate moans from his tortuous attacks.

This powerful man was seriously killing me.

"Stop." I muttered under my breathless pants, feeling his smooth hands gently cupping my bra.

He stopped what he was doing and looked up with a knowing smirk. "What did you say, baby?" He taunted, wrapping an arm around my waist.

He pulled me closer, forcing my eyes to meet his.

His breath fanned my face while his eyes lingered on my lips before they returned back to my eyes.

I looked away, unable to meet his eyes which had a powerful glow in them. It was as if he was fuming because of what I had said.

"Say it again, baby." He smirked, lightly pulling my chin to face him while I swallowed my saliva in anxiousness.

"I want you to stop, boss." I croaked out, trying my best to calm myself down.

At my words, he leaned back against his seat and entwined his fingers together on his laps.

His eyes continued to watch me as I scrambled to my feet and adjusted my bra.

My hands moved to his desk to grab my blouse when his firm ones swooped down and caught mine.

I directed my gaze towards him and found myself moving to his lead as he placed it above his crotch.

There was a huge bulge underneath which was slowly standing at attention.

Sh*t, I got him turned on.

"Look at what you've been doing to me, baby. And you want me to stop?"

I gulped, withdrawing my hand from his crotch.

Turning around, I quickly hid my embarrassment and donned my blouse.

I was about to take a step forward and escape from this hell hole when his voice stopped me.

"I won't stop until I get what I want."

+++

It has been a week since he ignored me. I was more happier this way.

He would have frequent visits from women wearing tight dresses or wearing just a trench coat with nothing else inside.

That was how he had spent his week for the first time since I worked for him.

He would usually keep it low and visit pubs to look for women.

But somehow, I had a feeling that he was doing all these just to spite me.

Who cares anyways? As long as he doesn't try to screw me up again, I'm perfectly fine.

I arranged the stacks of the files neatly and stood up as I walked towards his office.

Pray hard that he was not having sex right now. I shivered at the thought.

Curling my fingers around the cooling metal handle, I pushed past the door and felt myself silently gasping at the sight.

Boss was seated on a comforter. His thighs were spread apart with a woman kneeling in between his thighs.

His eyes shot open and found mine as he smirked at me. His grip on the brunette's hair tightened as he pushed her head closer to his aroused d*ck.

His eyes stayed on me the entire time as his orgasm came.

With both feet stood rooted to the ground, I felt my body betrayed me when I wanted to turn and leave.

But, I just couldn't bring myself to do it.

The woman whipped her head towards my direction and jumped slightly in shock.

Her lips were smeared with semen with her perky breasts on full view.

She was wearing a short skirt while her blouse was on the floor.

"Wipe off the semen from your mouth and wipe them on your breasts for her to see." He ordered, eyeing me as I watched with my eyes wide open.

What the f*ck was he trying to do?

+++

Vote. Comment. Share

Enjoying this book? Add this book to your library and your reading list.

8th August 2016

8: Calling The Shots

The woman did what she was told, wiping the semen on her perky breasts in front of me. I grimaced at the sight, silently swearing to myself.

What the f*ck was he trying to do?

"Alright, that's enough. Leave, Mandy." He said, smirking as the woman did what she was told and left the office in a hurry.

He stood up, pulling up the zip before resting his eyes on me. Mischief flickered across his lust filled orbs as he stared at me.

"Did you see that, Natalie? Every woman I have sex with, will do what I say." He murmured, sliding his hand down my thigh while I shuddered involuntarily.

He surprised me by pushing me against his desk, both arms trapping my sides. "And why is it so hard when it comes to you, baby?"

As he whispered, his fingers parted my thighs and stuck a finger into my moist entrance. "So wet for me, baby." He purred huskily, sliding his finger out as he slipped it into his mouth.

His desire grew as he stared at me while I was trying my hardest not to fall for his trap. What his naughty fingers could do was like spreading a whiff of love potion, making me see things in a blur.

But I didn't want all of it, knowing that he was purely lusting over my body. I just wanted an escape from this man who could easily manipulate me.

"So what do you say, baby?" He prompted, slowly kissing his way up my neck. "No." I wheezed out, looking away.

The warmth of his body against mine left me as he walked towards his glass window. His broad back faced me, looking so big as compared to my petite figure.

"Leave." It was all I needed as I left the files on his desk and hurriedly pulled down my skirt before leaving the office like as if I hadn't left for years.

+++

Pulling up by the curb, I sighed as I removed my helmet and sauntered my way through the arena like I had done it for a million times.

Walking into the room where I used to go during Pitbull's previous match-es, I was met with a top half naked boss as his eyes rested on mine.

Clearing my throat, I took a glance at his hands before making my way to the first aid kit as I pulled out the bandages.

I moved towards him, slowly lifting his hand as I tied the bandage over his knuckles, making sure that it wasn't too tight before fastening the ends.

Moving on to his next hand, I ignored his burning stares while I tried my hardest to focus on his hand than on him.

Today at work was a real fiasco and he hasn't bothered to talk to me ever since. Like I have said, I really don't mind. The problem was him and his lust over my body.

When I was done, I let his hand drop to his side before spinning on my heels to move away from him. I was planning to stay in this room until his match was over.

Arms wrapped around my waist as he pulled me towards him. I gasped, clasping my hands over his to remove it.

His breath fanned my neck as he leaned against me. "I want to see you there when I fight, baby." He whispered, kissing his way up my neck.

I nodded, pulling away from him as I sat down on the bench and looked away. A man knocked on the door before entering with a clipboard under his arm.

"The match is starting soon. Please get ready, Viper." He announced before walking off. I looked up to be met with his eyes as he took one last glance of me before leaving for his next match.

+++

Vote. Comment. Share

Enjoying this book? Add this book to your library and your reading list.

15th August 2016

9: The Match

Mixing myself in the crowd, my ear drums were almost damaged due to the deafening screams of the crowd in the arena when Viper had made his appearance.

Stopping at the ring, he lifted his hoodie and let it dropped to the ground. I could have sworn that the crowd had increased their volumes at the sight.

I watched as his steady breathing began slow as his eyes matched the venomous glares of his opponent, Hunter.

Hunter, standing at six feet tall, was a few inches shorter than Declan, but his agility was unmistakable. Even Pitbull who rarely gave praises had once complimented him when the match between them was over.

Maybe, this fight might determine if he had met his match. It would be a fight worth watching.

The bell went off, signalling that the match had started. Both competitors began circling each other in the ring as they waited for the right opportunity to arrive.

A blow merely missed Declan's face as he blocked it with his elbow. He attacked back with a punch and a few kicks in the stomach until he fell to the ground.

His foot made contact with the soft surface of the ring as Hunter rolled over and got up to his feet in a millisecond.

He retaliated back by kicking his knee which sent him moving a few steps back before a blow was sent to Hunter's face.

He blinked a few times at the impact before another blow flew to his face.

Seeing that he was walking back unstably, Declan grabbed the opportunity and kicked his stomach repeatedly with his nails digging into his flesh of his broad shoulders as he stopped him from moving.

Hunter glared at him as he clenched his jaws while trying to struggle under his iron grip.

Blood spurted from his mouth as he hung his head forward before a blow was sent to his face with the referee blowing the whistle, signalling that the match was over.

Hunter laid unconscious on the ground with his face smeared with his own blood.

My eyes met his wandering eyes which landed solely on me. Many heads were whipped in my direction while some females glared at me in jealousy.

I swallowed a bile which was rising to my throat and looked away, slowly making my way back to the room as images of him fighting so seriously flooded my mind.

He always wore that face when he was in a serious mode. It was a face that I would tend to notice whenever I was in his office before the whole 'I-want-to-f*ck-you' thing started.

I could never know how many faces he had. Wouldn't he be tired of choosing faces to show to people?

The door flung open as I looked up to see Declan trudging into the room with a solemn look.

My eyes rested on his bandages wrapped around his fists which was soaked with blood.

I stood up, reaching over for the first aid kit before pulling him onto the bench as I began to work on his wounds.

As I was carefully peeling away the bandages, I could feel his burning gaze which got me really tensed.

Ignoring it, I continued to apply antisceptic cream on his wounds before wrapping them up in bandages.

I proceeded to check if there was any injury on any part of his body, eventually heaving a sigh of relief when all was intact.

Imagine him to be Hunter who was laid on the ground unconscious. I wouldn't dare to sleep well at the sight.

Wait, what the f*ck was I thinking? Why should I even be worried for him? He had attempted to f*ck me a couple of times.

As I kept away the first aid kit, I was pulled into his arms as his warm eyes stared back at mine.

"Declan?" I croaked out, feeling his forehead resting against mine as he closed his eyes.

"Just let me feel your warmth." He murmured with a soft voice. I pursed my lips into a thin line, keeping quiet.

We stayed in this position for as long as I could remember.

+++

"Bring in the materials I have requested and make sure that no one enters the office for the next half an hour." He spoke through the intercom from the phone connected between us while I complied.

Sorting out the files he had requested, I carried them as I approached his office.

Pushing past the door, my gaze followed to the man who had tried to get in my pants. He must be here for the collaboration again.

Interestingly, his PA was not with him.

I walked towards the couch and placed the files on the coffee table, feeling holes burning on my chest as I looked up to see him smirking at me.

A cough caught his attention as he looked away from me and smiled at boss who was, on the other hand, looking very pissed off.

Ignoring it, I bowed before making a quick escape out of the office before things gets even more awkward.

+++

Vote. Comment. Share

Enjoying this book? Add this book to your library and your reading list.

22th August 2016

10: Hesitation

Two hours rolled by quickly and both CEOs had just ended their meeting. As boss stepped out of his office to send him off, Mr. Anderson's eyes found mine as he winked at me.

I bowed politely, though thoroughly disgusted with his stares, especially on my cleavage.

While boss was, on the other hand, trying to keep his cool as he sent him until the lobby.

I turned my attention back to the task at hand and occupied myself with the load of work awaiting me.

As I was too engrossed in the admin work, I did not even realise that boss was standing beside my desk, watching me.

I looked up, jumping in fright at his presence as his lips tilted up into a smirk.

Bending forward slightly, he lifted my chin to match his gaze before locking lips.

I gasped, surprised by his actions as I tried to push him away. He pulled me up with him and had me pinned against the desk in seconds with my wrists in his tight grip.

Pulling away, his hungry gaze raked across my body as my face heated up.

This was too much.

"Going to refuse me again?" He stated dryly, smirking at my astonished reaction. I gulped, swallowing my saliva.

I wasn't going to like where this sh*t was heading to.

"I won't touch you, until you beg me for it." He paused, rubbing circles on my inner thigh as I bit back a moan. "But that doesn't mean that you're not mine, because you belong to me."

Gritting my teeth, I murmured in a rage, "Never in your wildest dreams, Declan."

Hoping that my words would make him give up, I didn't expect that his smirk would grow wider.

"We shall see about that, babe."

++++

I walked into the lounge and began to make a cup of coffee to wake my dying brain.

That stupid boss had given me a pile of admin work to complete, said that the deadline was tomorrow.

He was deliberately trying to kill me with this sh*t. Was this his way of making me beg him to touch me?

That will never happen.

Walking back to my desk in a state of drowsiness, I took in a few sips of the coffee before keeping my eyes trained on the screen in front of me.

This was going to be a long night.

++++

After hours of hard work, my work was eventually completed as I began to stretch my limbs.

Whipping my head towards the clock, my eyes widened when I realised that it was half past three in the morning.

It would be no use heading home since I only had a few hours to sleep before reporting for work in the morning.

Boots hit the polished floor as boss emerged from the shadows. He checked his watch before looking at me.

"It seems to me that you have no choice but to stay over." He said with a smirk tugged on his lips.

"It's fine. I will sleep here."

My eyes widened at his next sentence, "No, you will sleep in my room."

"You are crazy. Why would I even sleep in your room?" I stated the obvious, almost yelling at him.

He simply chuckled, shaking his head in amusement. "If you're worried about sleeping in the same bed as me, you don't have to worry about that. I am taking the couch tonight."

I let out a sigh and bobbed my head up and down in response. He spun on his heels and walked back to his office while I followed behind him.

He threw me his oversized top and a pair of boxers, motioning towards the bathroom. I complied and quickly stripped as I took a quick bath.

When I was done, I squeezed my wet hair and slipped on the oversized top without a bra.

Like hell would I care if he would see. I was simply too tired to fight with him.

Folding my arms, I reappeared into his room just as he had pulled a shirt over his head.

He turned around as if sensing my presence, smirking at me. "You look sexy as hell in my shirt." He commented, raking his eyes across my body before resting on my folded arms where I was hiding my bare breasts.

"I will return you after I have washed it." I replied, looking away as my face heated up.

He didn't say anything else, but laid on the couch while I slipped under the sheets and shut my eyelids.

I was comfortable in this position, until arms were wrapped around my waist, alerting me that there was someone else.

Declan. Again.

++++

Vote. Comment. Share

Enjoying this book? Add this book to your library and your reading list.

29th August 2016

11: Why Can't You?

When I opened my notifications, I was shocked with the overwhelming votes and books added to reading lists! It really made this week the best week of my life And shockingly, we have reached 10k+ reads! So here's an early update to celebrate. Please enjoy ;)

I shivered involuntarily, clasping my hands over his warm ones and tried to pull them away from my waist.

However, it was redundant. He just wouldn't budge.

Pretty annoying.

"Declan." I groaned in frustration, hitting his legs with mine to get him to move.

"Hush, baby. Just let me hug you in this position." He whispered, his breath fanning my left ear.

"Why?"

His arms around my waist tightened incredibly, though he did gave me some space to breathe.

His lips made contact with my exposed shoulder blade where the large shirt I was wearing had uncovered some portion of my skin.

I froze instantly, blinking furiously as I tried to regain my senses.

What the sh*t was going on? My emotions were flying all over the place.

I was feeling a mix of bliss and confusion.

"I am confused with myself." He stated which made me open my mouth to say something when his nose ran down the nape of my neck.

I shuddered slightly, hesitating whether to ask what he had meant by those words.

What could possibly make him be confused with himself? What made him think this way?

"Why are you... confused with yourself?" I asked, licking my lips as I tasted my chapped lips.

"Your mere presence makes me feel that way."

Shocked at his words, I gulped and felt my breath hitched at the back of my throat.

"Stop, I don't want to listen anymore." I whispered, covering my ears as I panicked.

He was manipulating my mind again. All the trouble for just a simple f*ck.

No, I won't ever be affected by his words. I won't let him have what he wants.

"Why can't you-" I closed my eyes at his words and covered the duvets over my head, covering my ears tightly.

Ignoring everything he had said, I thought about the good things instead.

A new car, preferably Camry brand or a studio apartment nearby.

Just by thinking about the good things in life, I was able to distract myself from what he was saying.

He was definitely saying things that would manipulate my innocent mind.

And he would have the chance to f*ck me and throw me away like a used toy.

Insecure was all I felt, as long as I was around him.

++++

Waking up the next morning, I threw the covers off my face and groaned, shifting to the side.

Leaning my temple against my clasped hands, I found a comfortable spot which lulled me to sleep once again.

Wait. If it was morning, wouldn't I have work to do?

Opening my eyes, I adjusted to the light in the room before figuring out where I was.

Office.

Room.

Bed. Wait, bed?

My eyes widened as I took in the sight of the room in a blurry state, slowly sitting up.

"Awake?" I snapped my head towards the right, upon hearing a husky voice.

Boss who was seated on the armchair was watching me with a hint of amusement.

Rubbing my face, I raked my fingers across my hair and yawned in an unladylike manner.

"I suppose you had a good sleep with me by your side the entire night." He stated, still watching me as I stretched my limbs.

Rolling my eyes, I mumbled, "Dream on." before my eyes landed on the shopping bag on the edge of the bed.

"I'm assuming that's mine." I said, inching my way towards the shopping bag as I pulled out the outfit.

Surprisingly, the pencil skirt was longer than the previous ones he had bought.

"What's with the sudden change in my attire?" I asked teasingly, looking at him who had a nonchalant look on his face.

"Didn't someone said that I should show off my curves more often?"

"That's when you're with me. No one is allowed to look at your curves except for me." He growled in a possessive manner as he stood up.

"But I'm only choosing this attire as we're going to meet Mr. Anderson at the construction site to oversee the project." He said, slowly walking towards me until he was in front of me.

He bent down and leveled his eyes with mine, staring at me with a hint of... concern?

"And I don't want him to make a move on you. So you have to be by my side at all times."

I stared at him in utter shock. He was actually concerned about me.

++++

Vote. Comment. Share

Enjoying this book? Add this book to your library and your reading list.

31st August 2016

12: Protective Mode

After having a good bath, I reapplied my makeup with a few finishing touches and I was good to go.

As I walked out of his room connected to his office, he was seated down on the couch with conjoined hands as he stared at me.

His eyes watched me lustfully as I walked towards him confidently. His eyes raked across my figure, checking me out openly.

Blush crept up to my cheeks as I looked down at what I was wearing which consists of a velvet silk blouse with ruffles in the middle and a black pencil skirt.

However, the blouse was a little tight such that my breasts protruded out in an obvious way.

Sh*t, I just remembered that Mr. Anderson loved to check out my boobs. Oh no, what should I do?

"Don't worry about that man. I will make sure that he doesn't lay a finger on you." He assured, standing up as he grabbed his blazer from the seat.

"Put it on for me, babe." He whispered, staring at me intensely.

I obliged, swallowing my saliva as I took the blazer and put it on for him. As I was adjusting his collar, I could feel his fingers tracing down my spine with a gentle touch.

His fingers reached my ass and groped it, wrapping my legs around his waist swiftly.

I gasped at the sudden move and stared at him before feeling his lips pressed against mine.

Slowly wrapping my arms around his neck, I let him devour me with his body pressed tightly against mine.

As each second passed, our kiss slowed down with either one of us panting for breath.

The moment his fingers made its way towards my inner thighs where it was almost reaching my womanhood, I broke away from the kiss I had responded to and pushed him away.

I can't believe that I had actually willingly kissed him like that. I shouldn't even allow my determination to waver.

Spinning on my heels, I rushed out of his office quickly. This was the most embarrassing moment ever.

I was going crazy soon.

++++

Walking behind boss, I took note of the details of the construction site, especially the hazardous areas.

If we have to get into somewhere deeper in the site, we have to be alert and cautious at all times.

But, I must admit that this place was spacious enough to get lost if it was a maze.

That was what I was afraid of since I wasn't very familiar of this place.

"Mr. Connor." We turned around to see Mr. Anderson walking towards us with a man who had a clipboard under his arm.

He must be the contractor.

"Nice to meet you, Mr. Connor." The man greeted, shaking hands with boss while I could feel a burning gaze on my chest.

Looking towards my left, Mr. Anderson was staring intensely at my chest.

Covering up my chest, I pulled the blazer around my body even tighter than before.

He took a step towards me when boss and the contractor weren't looking while I stood there, hoping this sh*t would end soon.

Boss turned towards us, his eyes resting on something before striding towards me as he pulled me towards him.

"Derrick, you aren't giving me face if you continue to do this." He stated, his voice going dangerously lower as he stared at him.

I gulped, leaning against him for support as Mr. Anderson merely chuckled, brushing him off.

"Alright, I won't." He assured, his eyes shifting towards me as he smirked charmingly before walking towards the contractor.

I sighed, taking a few steps back. "Are you okay?" Boss asked, worry written all over his face.

I nodded furiously, trying to calm down. "I'm fine, we should go." I stated, slowly walking behind them as I tried not to let my knees buckle before me.

Mr. Anderson's fingers almost touched my ass. And I didn't like it one bit.

At least, Declan could give me the satisfaction. Wait, what was I thinking?

I was really going to go bonkers soon.

++++

Vote. Comment. Share

Enjoying this book? Add this book to your library and your reading list.

5th September 2016

13: Falling Deep

"**I**f there's any changes to be made, inform my PA and we can work things out on our next meeting."

The contractor nodded his head in response as he turned towards Mr. Anderson while exchanging a few words with him.

Boss strode towards me and whispered against my ear," We're going back. I'm sending you home."

Ignoring how his breath sent a chill down my spine, I opened my lips to say something but shut them instead, pouting as we walked the rest of the way to his car.

Hesitatingly, I entered the back seat as the chauffeur started driving. I could feel his intense stare on me as I tried hard to control my urges.

I don't know why, but I felt sexually aroused than ever as the engine beneath us roared to life.

The wheels hit something hard, making me jump in my seat as my skirt was pushed up my thighs.

I gasped, quickly pulling down the hem of my skirt as I closed my legs together, feeling the wetness from my v-line.

Sh*t, what was happening to me?

My eyes flickered to his burning gaze as he continued to stare at me.

I turned my gaze to my skirt, fiddling with my fingers instead.

All of a sudden, there was a screech from the car as it turned to its left, sending me flying towards boss as I straddled his torso.

His eyes continued to watch me as his lips tilted up into a smirk.

Panicking, I tried to move away from him when he grabbed hold of my waist and kept me in place.

"Boss, please let me go." I pleaded, feeling my heart leaping out of my lungs as I took in large gulpes of breath.

He said nothing, but continued to watch me as he pushed my skirt up to my waist and groaned in delight.

"You're wet for me, aren't you?" He teased, tugging on my thongs as he slid a finger in.

Gasping, I tried to struggle again but ended up in a moaning mess as his finger circled my clit.

He pulled it out and licked the wet juices, the look in his eyes were as though he was tasting me.

His lust-filled orbs stared into mine as I figured that mine was mirroring him as well.

He shot a smirk of his own as he slid two fingers under my thongs and thrusted in, making me gasp as another moan escaped from my lips.

His fingers continued to circle my clit until I was almost reaching my climax. My body responded to him as he continued to pleasure me with his skillful fingers.

As I was about to reach the climax, he pulled his fingers out and slid them into his mouth, licking off all of my wet juices.

Through my glazed orbs, I groaned when he didn't continue.

"Boss." I groaned aloud in frustration, grinding my hips against his for more.

"Have you finally come around?" He whispered, my body pressed against his tightly.

My body betrayed me and reacted to him as I continued to grind my hips against his. His lips made contact with my neck as he left open-mouthed kisses.

I moaned when his lips found my sensitive spot as he grazed his teeth across it, slowly leaving behind a love bite of his own.

The car suddenly came to a stop as my body continued to be pressed against his with his hungry lips attacking mine.

He continued to devour me as his fingers raked across my ponytail and tugged my hair tie down with ease.

He pulled back for a moment to look at me while I felt blush creeping up to my cheeks. "You look beautiful with your hair down, babe." He whispered, playing with my hair before smashing my lips with his.

++++

Vote. Comment. Share

Enjoying this book? Add this book to your library and your reading list.

12th September 2016

14: Pressing On

His tongue tangled with mine, pressing my body even tighter against his.

Each second passed with his lips pressed against mine was heaven.

It was then did I felt nostalgic. It was as though I had kissed those lips before.

His hands roamed around my body while he groaned when I was doing a good job in pleasuring him.

His lips hungrily devoured mine, biting and sucking my lips until they turned swollen.

God, he was making me so addicted.

Yet, the only thing I couldn't capture was his face. If only I could remember it during the night I was drunk...

Slowly regaining my senses, I pushed him away immediately and looked away.

Our pants filled the car, even his chauffeur had already gotten out to give us privacy.

"Sorry, we-we can't do this." I stuttered, grabbing my handbag when I noticed that we had reached my house.

He gripped my wrist, halting me from leaving as my hand on the door handle loosened slightly.

"Wait-" He was interrupted by his phone ringing which made me sigh in relief.

Saved by the phone call.

I looked towards him with a smile, removing his hand from my wrist and quickly got out of the car.

Without looking back, I brisk-walked to the lobby and hastily got into the lift.

Resting a palm on my chest, I breathed in heavily in hopes of calming myself down. My heart was beating erratically which was turning me berserk soon.

Why was I even feeling this way when all he wanted was just simply a f*ck?

Oh god, please don't tell me that I have fallen in love with him.

++++

Skimming my lips across the rim of the glass, I downed another glass of whiskey.

After a few rounds of shots, my cheeks must be flaming red right now.

Anyways, since it was the weekends already, I could use a drink or two, now that I was so confused with my feelings.

Eyeing the glass in my hands, I imagined his lips against mine as his hands slowly roamed around my body.

Our bodies pressed against each other while I grinded my hips against his with a seductive smirk.

Now, I was the one who was mad. Oh god, I must be really mad.

I can't believe I would actually be thinking about this. The heels of my palms kissed my forehead as I groaned aloud, obviously unaware of a presence behind me.

It was until the chair squeaked beside me did I looked up to see him ordering a drink from the bartender.

Why was boss here? Oh wait, maybe he was looking for a woman to satisfy him.

No matter how much my confidence level had plunged down, I would never agree to do it with him.

Turning back to my glass of whiskey, I downed another shot, the liquid burning my throat.

"Hey, handsome." An alluring voice rang in my ears as I watched from the peripheral of my vision where a woman was already hitting on him.

Seems like someone was getting his victim on his bed tonight.

My face, however, wore a scowl as she whispered sweet nothings to him, openly flirting with him.

My fingers around my glass tightened until I heard him muttering, "I'm with this woman here."

Snapping my head towards his direction, he shot me his infamous smirk while the woman scowled at me and stalked off in her 6 inches high stilettos.

Seriously, what's wrong with women wearing such high heels when it was obviously damn uncomfortable?

"Jealous that she has a pair of sexy legs than you?" He teased, noticing my eyes stayed fixated on her legs.

I glared at him, closing my eyes briefly in the hopes of lessening the pounding headache.

Oh no, I was seriously not going to look forward to a hangover tomorrow morning.

"You're drunk, babe." He stated, leaving a few notes on the table and carried me in bridal style.

Too weak to protest, I allowed him to carry me out of the bar.

He slipped into his car, holding me close towards him while he adjusted himself in a more comfortable position.

I was pretty much pressed up against him in a drunken state with my arms hanging around his neck loosely.

"Why did you drink so much, babe?" He murmured after the wheel hit the roads.

"I am pretty sure that's none of your concern, boss." I stated with an eye roll.

He chuckled, "Then you must be sober enough to retort me."

"That's because you're asking a senseless question."

"Is someone on her period?" He asked with a cheeky grin. I smiled slightly at his question and shook my head.

"You should be running far away from me if I am having my period right now."

"In that case, I don't mind a little cuddle to cool you down." He said, planting a soft kiss on my forehead.

"Do you always do that to other women?" I blurted out, surprised at my own choice of words.

"No, you're the second woman I have done that to, besides my mom." He replied while I felt blush creeping up to my cheeks in an instant.

I can't help but to let a smile spread across my face at his words. It was just a silly kiss on the forehead and I had gotten so girly like a high school teen.

I should have grown out of all those prince charming fantasies.

++++

Vote. Comment. Share

Enjoying this book? Add this book to your library and your reading list.

19th September 2016

15: Hangover

The sunlight burned my eyes the moment I woke up, finding myself curled up in bed sheets.

Pushing off the bed sheets, I felt my body feeling cold all of a sudden as I looked down, only to realise that I was only in my lace bra and thongs.

For god's sake, what did I do? Last night, I was drunk and couldn't remember anything, except that my boss had sent me home.

Looking around the room carefully, I realised that this wasn't my room.

Then, where the hell was I?

The door creaked open and boss came into view. His eyes raked across my body while I scrambled to grab the sheets to cover my body.

Was he the one who took off my clothes? "If you're thinking whether I had taken off your clothes last night, it's a 'no'. My maid did the job for me when you threw up all over my shirt."

"Did I? I'm sorry." I smiled sheepishly, scratching my nape in embarrassment.

He smirked, leaning forward with his eyes twinkling with mischief. "That's not all, babe. You have done something much worse."

Those words made my eyes widen in shock, my mind quickly processing his words. I did something worse than throwing up all over his shirt?

Closing my eyes briefly to ignore the pounding headache, I tried to think what I have done.

By the time I looked up, he was already standing by the door. "Wash up, babe. Breakfast is ready." And with that, he walked out of the room, leaving me in a state of confusion.

What had I done?

++++

Smoothening down the flares of the dress he had provided, I slowly made my way out of the room, only to be met with the sight of endless hallways.

Turning down corners after corners, I finally found the stairs which led me down to the foyer.

Clanking of pots and pans filled the room while I followed the sound where it led me to the kitchen.

It was certainly huge.

His back faced me while I watched as his muscles flexed when he moved his arms to get something.

"I know that my back view is simply too gorgeous not to stare. Why don't you sit down and eat while you can stare all day long?" His cocky remarks irked me as I groaned aloud.

"You're too full of yourself, Declan." I responded, sitting down on a bar stool as I looked down at my plate.

It was filled with scrambled eggs, sausages and toasts. Just by the sight of it made my mouth water.

I felt fingers bringing up my chin to face him as I frowned deeply. I hated it when someone interrupt me while I was appreciating something, especially when it has to do with food.

"Say my name again, babe." He whispered, carrying me up until my ass kissed the cooling polished counter.

"Boss." I gasped as I felt his crotch hitting my inner thighs.

He smirked, "Wrong answer."

I gasped again when I felt his fingers skimming down my thighs with mischief twinkling in his eyes.

He was making me so weak in front of him and I really hated myself for it. I was slowly going to succumb to him and submit to this beautiful creature.

"Declan." I breathed out heavily while he smirked, his fingers going further down until it reached the straps of my thongs where my core was already wet.

He closed his eyes briefly, groaning aloud. "I love it when you moan my name," He paused, opening his eyes just as he stuck a finger into my wet pussy.

"I want you so much, babe." He breathed out, kissing his way down my neck as his finger continued to plunge into my moist entrance.

"Declan." I groaned aloud, feeling my thongs pulled down my thighs just as a tongue entered my entrance.

His tongue circled my clit, teasing me endlessly while I tangled my fingers with his hair and tugged on it harshly as I wanted more.

I moaned his name again and again, arching my back forward as I climaxed. His tongue lapped up my wet juices, licking it all away while I moaned again.

Orgasming never felt so good. It felt even better when it was him giving me this feeling.

And I must be mad to have fallen into his honey trap. Yet, it felt so good with his hands on my body.

In fact, I wanted more.

++++

Vote. Comment. Share

Enjoying this book? Add this book to your library and your reading list.

26th September 2016

16: Caving In

A /N _ It's time for some real action *smirks*

[Mature contents]

Without hesitation, I slammed my lips against his, feeling the moisture of my wet v-line against his rough lips.

Tangling my fingers in his hair, I moaned into his mouth, my breathing hastening.

He slowly broke away from the kiss, wrapping my legs around his hips as he carried me up the flight of stairs.

Our eyes met with a glint of lust found in his dark orbs. I wanted him and so did he.

The urges were too difficult for me to ignore this time.

I felt my back hitting something soft and realised that I was laid on his bed.

He hovered above me, claiming my lips while his hand roamed around my body to his greatest content.

I arched my back forward, letting out a moan as he tore away the dress along with my bra.

His mouth latched onto one of my breasts, his tongue circling my nipple which was slowly hardening.

As he played with my breasts, visions of what happened the other night when I was drunk came back to me.

This scene was so familiar as if I had been there before. It couldn't be just a dream.

What if he was the guy who took away my virginity that eventful night?

It all made sense why he had found an interest in me because he was the one who f*cked me when both of us were drunk.

My senses were all lost when he stuck two fingers into my moist entrance. His fingers thrusted in and out again, sending me soaring again in ecstasy.

"Declan." This earned a groan from him.

Before I could come, he pulled out and took a step back, slowly stripping off his clothes.

I watched with a pained expression as I was on the verge of coming while taking in a sharp intake of breath as he stood in his naked glory.

I gasped, finding the scar on his right arm so familiar.

Oh my god, he was the one.

His fingers caressed my cheeks, concern spread all over his face.

"Are you okay? Are we going too fast?" He asked while I shook my head in response.

He took it as an answer to continue and traced his 10 inches shaft along my wet clit. Arching my back forward, I grinded my hips against his for more.

In a rush, he plunged down through my entrance, sending pleasures down my body.

Giving me time to adjust, he started thrusting in and out in a slow pace before his speed hastened.

A course of pleasure came rushing through my veins, sending me soaring in ecstasy.

"Declan." I moaned again, feeling a smile formed on his lips against my skin.

It was ironic how he was able to make me feel this way even after we had done it before a few years back.

I gasped, "More."

At my words, he roughly slammed his hips against mine while my walls clenched tightly for him.

"F*ck, you are so tight." He wheezed out, gripping my hips to control his thrusts.

He repeated for a few more times before we could feel our climax coming. As if on cue, my wet juices spilled all over his shaft while his hot seeds shot through my core.

We panted for breath, sweat trickling down our body as we stared at each other under the comfortable silence.

He pulled out, laying down beside me as he wrapped his arms around my body.

My fingers slowly traced his scar down his arm, looking into his eyes. "You are the guy that night, aren't you?"

His eyes closed briefly before opening them as though he was processing my words.

With a gentle nod, he gave me a peck on my lips and smiled. "I knew you were that woman ever since you stepped into my office. I have been noticing you ever since."

++++

Vote. Comment. Share

Enjoying this book? Add this book to your library and your reading list.

3rd October 2016

17: Lies And Deception

A/N _ I feel that I am an evil author.

It has been a week ever since we had sex together. He has been busy with his work, and so was I.

Apparently, the construction work for the project has started and things were getting bumpy for the past few days which made work more sufferable for me.

Scrolling down the emails, I sighed as I checked every one of them which was mostly about the incident that the supplies received had something wrong and had to return back to the suppliers.

Right now, the problems were resulting in the project to be postponed to a later date.

And the most funny thing was, we literally had no time to talk to each other.

It was unusual.

No matter how busy he was, he would always find a way.

Unless he was avoiding me after he had gotten what he wanted.

Have I fallen into his trap by giving him what he wanted and getting betrayed, dumped in the end?

God damn it, can things get any better?

The phone connected to the boss's office rang as I answered it.

"I need you in the office right now."

I pushed myself off the chair and began to walk towards the direction of the office,

With shaky hands, my fingers made contact with the metal handle as I pushed past the door.

Immediately, Boss had me pinned against the wall. His fingers tightened around my wrist as he pressed his body against mine.

His nose found his way to my neck as he bit my earlobe teasingly. "God, I missed you so much." He whispered.

Instantly, my hands found its way to his chest as I pushed him away.

I was seeing red right now. He has been avoiding me, and now he was telling me that he missed me?

Was this kind of joke or something?

"Stop lying in my face, Declan. Admit it, you have been avoiding me." I wheezed out, feeling my veins popping out as anger coursed through them.

He kept silent.

And, I knew that I was right. Darn it, I was so right this time.

I shouldn't have trusted him.

I turned on my heels as I walked away. Tears seeped out of my tear ducts uncontrollably as I wanted to dig out a hole and hide in there for my entire life.

I can't believe that I was so stupid to have actually trusted a man like him.

Walking out of the building, I hadn't realised that it was having a downpour.

Ignoring the rain, I continued to make my way down the pavements as I walked home.

Since my motorbike was currently under maintenance, I had to walk home instead.

A gush of cold wind blew past me as I pulled the jacket tighter towards me.

Droplets of rain rolled down my face as it mixed well with the tears that were dripping down my cheeks.

Tears blurred my vision as I walked down the road aimlessly.

People rushing past me didn't affect me the slightest, I just continued walking with my body soaked in the heavy rain.

He was just my boss. What was I even expecting from him?

He was a player and a jerk. What use could it be if we were together?

Nothing. No matter what the result is, it would be nothing.

I was nothing to him, just a secretary used for his sexual needs.

I hated the feeling of being used. And I hated myself for letting him have the chance to use me for his sexual needs.

Turning the doorknob, I entered my apartment and immediately broke down with silent tears.

What I have hoped not to happen, eventually turned into a reality.

A horrible reality.

++++

Vote. Comment. Share

Enjoying this book? Add this book to your library and your reading list.

10th October 2016

18: Taken Cared Of

I woke up, feeling heavy and sick. God damn it, I was running a fever right now.

Shifting to the side, I pushed myself up and climbed out of bed.

No matter how sick I was, heartbroken I felt, company's matters were still important.

I can't fall sick, not when the project was still getting rocky.

And I wasn't going to let my feelings for him get the best of me.

Time will heal everything, I believe in that.

I sauntered into the bathroom and closed the door.

++++

Finding my will, I stepped into the office as I held onto the files in my arms tightly.

His eyes found mine while my heart raced even quicker.

Deciding to ignore it, I handed him the files and stood by the desk, waiting for him to check through the content.

As I waited, my head began to feel dizzy as I closed my eyes briefly.

By the time I opened them, he had placed down his pen as worry was plastered all over his handsome face.

"Are you okay, babe?" He asked while I snapped in frustration, "Don't call me that."

I sighed after realising what I had done. "I am sorry." I whispered meekly, taking the files in my hands as I walked out of his office.

Before I could even step out of his office, my limbs weakened as I felt my knees buckled before me.

The sound of footsteps came rushing towards me as I looked towards him in a blurry state.

His lips moved, mumbling words I couldn't hear before I felt everything went black.

++++

His fingers travelled down my rosy cheeks as he smiled charmingly. "You're so beautiful." He whispered in my ear while I giggled like a kid after a few drops of alcohol mixed in my system.

I knew that I shouldn't be drinking since I was a lousy drinker, but I just couldn't help myself since I have turned 21.

I was an adult now, and I should choose my own path, whether to lose my virginity to this guy in front of me.

My eyes flickered to his lips as I took a sharp intake of breath.

"I want to f*ck you so hard." He whispered again, this time nipping my earlobe as his fingers brushed past my neck.

I bit my lips, already making my decision. It was now or never. "Go ahead then."

I peeled my eyes open at the memory, taking in deep breaths to calm my racing heart down.

Slowly sitting up, I realised that my headache was gone.

My eyes wandered around the room I was in, finding myself in Boss's room.

God damn it, did he let me sleep in here?

The door creaked open as he entered the room with a tray in his hands.

His face lit up upon seeing me awake while my brows pulled together into a frown.

Has he been taking care of me all this time?

Climbing out of the bed, I stood up only to be faced with him.

Taking in a deep breath, I murmured, "Thank you for taking care of me, I will leave now."

As I tried to walk past him, his arm stopped me. I tried to push past him but to no avail.

He was too strong for me.

He laid the tray on the nightstand and pushed me onto the bed before climbing on top of me.

What the f*ck was he trying to do?

++++

Vote. Comment. Share

Enjoying this book? Add this book to your library and your reading list.

18th October 2016

19: He Tries Too Hard

His dark orbs stayed fixated on me. I felt my breath hitched at the back of my throat as I looked away.

My chest rose and fell erratically at the close proximity between us. It has been quite a long time since he touched me in a loving way.

But, I know that he was just trying to confuse me.

"Are you letting me go?" I asked, my voice hoarse from dehydration.

"No, I am not letting you go again." I tensed at his words, closing my eyes in disbelief.

"No matter how hard you try, it's not going to work between us." I snarled, pushing him off my body as I stood up.

I moved past the bed to the armchair and picked up my coat. Winter was coming and I needed that, especially when it has been raining every now and then.

If not for the seasonal rain, I wouldn't have got caught in the rain and caught a flu. It just made things worse, especially when he took care of me this whole time.

What was I thinking? I could have gotten an umbrella or something.

"Babe." He said, latching his hand on my arm to stop me.

I stayed in the same position with my back still faced him.

"Let me explain, I am not going to let you go again." He whispered earnestly while I rolled my eyes in response.

"Too late." I stated coldly, removing his hand from my arm as I left the room.

++++

I followed behind him, taking down notes while the contractor continued to speak.

He predicted that the completion of this project might be delayed until next year which also meant that more costs would be incurred since the project was already facing issues.

My eyes stayed fixated on his tensed back as he listened attentively to the contractor.

After that day, he has been cooped up in his office, working his ass off all day long.

It was only on rare occasions did he come out of that hell hole.

When he tried to strike a conversation with me while checking through the files, I would cut him off with many excuses.

The only contact between us was when I needed him to sign the files or when he needed me to prepare a meeting.

And the meetings these days became very common. The board of directors were concerned with this project as it would drag the company down.

And they were constantly requesting meetings with the boss. This made me incredibly busy and worn out.

I continued to take down notes until the contractor was finally done with his observations.

"Natalie, get the chauffeur to prepare my car in five minute's time." He said, not looking at me.

I nodded, keeping my notes as I called the chauffeur. Turning back to boss, I motioned towards the carpark.

"The car is ready." I said, chucking my phone back to my bag.

"I need a few words with the contractor, you head there first." He said, turning back to the contractor once more as he engrossed himself in a heavy conversation.

I sighed, walking ahead first where the chauffeur was already waiting for us.

As he opened the door for me, he murmured something that stopped me dead in my tracks.

"I can see that he is in love with you, he doesn't want to admit that he has feelings for you."

I shook my head in disbelief, "I find it too hard to believe."

And I got into the car and waited for him to arrive. While I waited, I thought of his words.

If he has feelings for me, why was he avoiding me in the first place? Why would he not want to admit that he has feelings for me?

He was a man whom I can never figure out what he's truly thinking.

That makes him even more dangerous.

++++

Vote. Comment. Share

Enjoying this book? Add this book to your library and your reading list.

25th October 2016

20: Confessions From A Drunk

As I got ready to sleep, the door knocked persistently.

It was raining heavily right now and I just wanted to coop inside my room all night.

Heaving a huge sigh, I climbed out of my bed and answered the door.

Surprisingly, it was boss.

He stood on my doorway, drenched from head-to-toe as he stumbled his way towards me

"Boss." I said, taking a step back as my eyes enlarged at the smell of alcohol.

He was drunk.

"You're drunk and you have came to the wrong place."

He chuckled, shaking his head. "I am very sober right now, babe. If I don't get to say what I want by tonight, I will not leave through this door."

I hissed, "I don't want to hear anything from you. Just leave."

"Just hear me out." He said through clenched teeth. I stood there frozen, staring at him.

"I thought that when I f*cked you, I will be able to forget you easily. Turns out, after that simple f*ck, it just made my life a whole lot worse." He paused, dragging his face down wearily.

"Everyday I am always thinking about you, I just can't get you off my mind."

He took a few steps towards me as he wrapped my petite figure in his arms.

"I may be a player, but I can't change the fact that I am madly in love with you, babe." He whispered against my ear, his hot breath fanning my neck.

I took a sharp intake of breath as I digested his words.

Why was my heart beating erratically? Why was I leaning into his touch unconsciously?

Have I also fallen in love with him as well?

I pulled away and glared at him through my thin eyelashes. "Why did you avoid me in the first place?"

He sighed, "I am confused with myself. I needed time to figure things out."

"And? What is your conclusion?" I urged, hoping the answer to be similar to what I wanted.

He raised his head to look at me. "I can't live a single day without you."

Instantly, my heart leapt out of my lungs as I smiled, leaning in as our lips met.

I moaned into his mouth as I wrapped my legs around his waist. Our lips molded against each other with passion and lust, the feeling I have missed for so long.

He laid me down onto the couch, his fingers skimming down my curves as he teased my bottom lips.

He pulled away, pecking my lips once more as he smiled. "I love you, babe."

A smile played on my lips as I blinked furiously. "I love you too."

"Good." He whispered against my skin, kissing his way down my neck.

I clamped my hands against his wet skin and groaned. "Can you at least get a bath?"

He pulled away and looked at me with a cheeky grin. "How about a bath with me?"

++++

I woke up to a sleeping Declan beside me. I can't help but to smile as I traced the features of his face softly.

Is this what it feels like to be in love?

As I was admiring his sleeping face, his hand reached out for my wrist as he peeled his eyelids open.

He shifted slightly towards me, kissing my knuckles. "What are you doing?" He asked huskily.

I smirked, "I am doing what a woman would do to her man."

He barked out a laugh, leaning in as he pecked my forehead.

His free hand reached up to my right cheek as he caressed my skin. "I don't mind waking up in this position every morning."

I looked down at our positions to see that our legs were tangled while our bodies were molded against each another.

I tilted up my head and shrugged casually, "I find it too warm."

"How about a cold bath instead?"

I narrowed my eyes into slits, "Didn't we bathed together last night?"

"We can save water again today." And with that, he carried me over his shoulder, spanking my ass cheeks in the process as he walked towards the bathroom.

What have I gotten myself into?

++++

Vote. Comment. Share

Enjoying this book? Add this book to your library and your reading list.

1st November 2016

21: A Date

I was checking through the recent emails when one of them caught my eye.

It was an invitation from the Anderson Cooperation. They have specially invited boss to make an appearance at their company dinner.

Since both companies were affiliated due to the project, boss might have to attend their events frequently.

And this was really bad news because I would have to tag along as his PA. Meeting Mr. Anderson again would be very unpleasant.

Can I apply leave on that day instead?

"Even if you try to, I'm not going to approve your leave." Boss's voice rang in my ears as I looked up to see him towering above me.

My eyes widened incredibly. "Did I say that out loud?" He simply smirked in response.

I pursed my lips into a thin line and sighed after a moment. "I just don't want to see him again in case he tries to..." I trailed off absentmindedly.

He clasped his hand over mine, squeezing it with reassurance. "I promise that I will never let him touch you."

A smile crept up to my lips as I nodded.

He checked his watch and smiled at me. "You are clocking off in five minute's time. Do I have the honor to bring you out for a date?"

I gasped in surprise. "A date?"

He nodded, holding onto my hand tightly as he led me to wherever he has planned for the date.

I didn't mind at all. Being with him was the perfect date I could ever ask for.

I stared at the sight before me as he extended his hand. He has brought me to his own private yacht and it was beautiful.

Climbing up the steps, I followed him as he led me to the inside where there was a lounge.

"This is so..." I trailed off, not knowing which word to use to describe the sight before me.

"Amazing?" He chimed in as I nodded, my eyes raking across the retro-styled lounge hungrily as though I have never seen one before.

Not that I have not seen one before, but most of them were from pictures found on Google.

I have always wanted to step inside a yacht to see how it feels like, more than just scrolling through pictures from the laptop.

He chuckled huskily, holding onto a shopping bag. "You might want to take a bath and get changed into this. We are spending the night here."

I took it and peered into the bag. "Why is it always you who gets to decide what I wear? And are these clothes really picked by you?"

He folded his arms, looking at me as though I was an intriguing piece. I bit my bottom lips and frowned, "Stop looking at me like that."

"Can't help it, babe. Just wear it, you will thank me later." He winked flirtatiously.

I huffed, not believing his words as I started making my way to the bathroom located at the side of the lounge.

Even the bathroom looked so extravagant and exquisite. However, the thing that catches my eyes the most was the bathtub.

++++

I re-entered the lounge to find it empty. Assuming that he was outside, I began to walk towards the exit.

The night breeze blew across my maxi skirt as I thanked the designer of this sweater.

If not for this sweater, I would have frozen to death by this chilly weather.

Seems like he was right. I would have to thank him for the clothes after all.

My eyes landed on his back as his blazer was removed and his sleeves were rolled up.

Wouldn't he be shivering by now?

I approached him, clearing my throat as he turned around with a glass of champagne in his right hand.

He took a few sips and raked his eyes across my figure. He placed his champagne down onto the marble coffee table and pulled me into his arms.

"You look beautiful as I had imagined."

As he said that, he tucked my hair behind my ears, a smile playing on his lips.

I raised a brow inquisitively, "Don't you have anything else to say, other than those compliments?"

++++

Vote. Comment. Share

Enjoying this book? Add this book to your library and your reading list.

8th November 2016

22: Worst Boyfriend Award? Maybe Not.

He laughed, his eyes twinkling in amusement. "What do you want me to say then? That I love you?"

I felt blush creeping up to my cheeks as my eyes wandered elsewhere but him.

Oh god, can he not be so blunt?

"Are you blushing?" He quirked an eyebrow while I looked down in embarrassment.

He chuckled huskily, kissing each of my red cheeks before stopping a few inches away from my lips.

His eyes flickered back to me with love in them. "I love you, babe."

"I-" I was cut off by his lips as he wrapped my legs around his broad hips.

I gasped, jolting awake for a moment before engrossing myself in the kiss. We began a heated make-out session, neither of us breaking the contact.

Eventually, I couldn't take it anymore and pulled away, panting heavily.

His hot breath fanned my neck as he tugged down my sweater to reveal my skin.

Instantly, I shivered at the chilly wind. He seemed to have noticed as he began walking in the direction of the entrance.

He threw me onto the bed, quickly making quick work of his pants as he slid himself inside of me.

I groaned, throwing my head to the back at the size of his.

Even though I was no longer a virgin, it still felt just like my first.

And he was the only man who could make me feel this way.

"Declan." I moaned, feeling his slams against my entrance as he greedily claimed my lips.

"Yes, baby." He whispered against my lips, grunting as he sent one last thrust.

Our release came at the same time, making a mess all over the sheets.

When we came down from our high, he rolled himself out of me and laid down beside me with a yawn in exhaustion.

My eyes noted his sunken eye bags as my thumb brushed past his skin. "Work must have taken a toll on you." I whispered, leaning against his chest.

He sighed, "Handling it by myself is fine, I don't want to tire you."

I looked up almost instantly in surprise, raising my brow. "That's why you have arranged this date?"

He nodded, conjoining his fingers with mine. "You deserve to relax a bit. You haven't been looking well lately."

A smile played on my lips at his words. "I'm surprised you have noticed that." I shrugged nonchalantly even though deep down, I was feeling rejoiced that he has spared a thought for me.

"If I haven't, I will probably be entitled the worst boyfriend ever." I laughed almost immediately, wrapping my arms around his waist.

"It doesn't matter, I love the way it is."

++++

He held onto my hand, walking along the concrete pavement with me.

He has ditched his car, his title, his suit in exchange for a life of an ordinary human being.

It was only for today since it was Friday. But, I didn't mind it at all because he was slowly changing for the sake of me.

My eyes rested on his polo shirt and brown pants, laughing at the sight. It was still funny seeing him wearing this, other than his suit.

His eyes met mine as he raised a brow inquisitively. "What's so funny?"

I shook my head, still in awe at this moment as I finally had a chance to see this version of him.

Not that I have fantasized before, but he should live like an ordinary human being for once.

We entered the supermarket. I grabbed a cart by the side and began pushing it.

He followed by the side, his eyes running through the different shelves.

"What are we getting today?" He asked, turning to look at me while I stared at the ceiling as I pondered through the items.

"Meat." He crossed his arms and raised a brow. "I have no idea where it is."

I rolled my eyes. "You're terrible. It's at the frozen section." I stated, pointing in the direction.

His lips parted, forming an 'o' shape. I chuckled, closing his lips for him before dragging him along with me.

He picked up a packet and showed it to me. "Is this the one?" He asked, raising a brow.

I huffed, a frown formed on my face instantly. "Look closely, it's a fish."

He chuckled huskily, chucking it to one side before picking up another packet which was similar to what I have in mind.

"I know that this is the meat you wanted, I was just fooling around." He winked flirtatiously while my jaws dropped to the ground, speechless at the sight before me.

Were my eyes working properly? Was this a playful version of him?

"Don't you like it?" He asked, pointing at the meat as I snapped out of my reverie.

I shook my head, taking it from him as I placed it on the cart.

"What a cute couple." A woman's voice attracted our attention as we turned to the side to see an old woman and an old man probably in their sixties looking at us.

I watched as Declan nodded, wrapping his arms around my waist as he pulled me close to him. "Thank you, I know we are."

Instantly, I rolled my eyes and smacked him, glaring at him at how shameless he was.

"I can't stand you." I tsked under my breath as he barked out a laugh.

"But I know you still love me."

++++

Vote. Comment. Share

Enjoying this book? Add this book to your library and your reading list.

15th November 2016

23: Company Dinner

C urling one last strand of my hair, I let it flow in waves as I eyed myself in the mirror.

I looked so different like as though I was getting married when it actual, it was for a company dinner.

Yet, the thought of meeting Mr. Anderson again terrified me. I was so afraid that he would try funny business with me again.

I hated the bad vibe it was giving me even before the event has started.

My phone made a noise in the middle of nowhere, startling me as I picked it up.

Reaching in five minutes, babe.

My brain recovered from the shock when I remembered that boss was my date today. He wanted to appear in this important occasion with me beside him.

This was a first time.

Slipping on my heels, I grabbed my keys and made a sprint for the door when I realised that I was almost late.

I don't want him waiting for me, or rather I would mind it if I let him wait for me for so long.

It just made me feel bad.

Just as I pushed past the door from the lobby, a familiar car pulled up in front of me.

He winded down the window, revealing a dashing Declan. I smiled, opening the door as I entered.

"You look like you were in a rush." He commented, turning down the volume slightly.

I straightened my back and sat properly. "Well, how can I make the boss wait for me?" I reasoned, trying to act like we were professionals.

"Stop that, babe. You are not being yourself at all."

I sighed, "It's so nerve-wrecking. I'm just nervous." I loosened down a little in front of him with a depressed look plastered on my face.

"Nervous of what?" He huskily asked, his eyes landing on me as they raked across the features of my face.

"Appearing beside you on this special occasion." I said, heaving a huge sigh as I swallowed a huge lump in my throat nervously.

He clasped his hand over mine as he pulled up by the gates.

Doomsday has arrived.

"Don't worry, I will be here for you." He reassured, squeezing my hand.

It was as though something kicked me that made me want to clear my bowels.

I must be getting too nervous right now.

Sitting up, I looked at him with an urgent look. "I need the washroom."

"Are you serious?" He asked with a hint of amusement flickering across his eyes.

I nodded, climbing out of the car as I quickly rushed through the entrance.

After getting out of the cubicle, I began to wash my hands just as a girl who was around eleven began counting her fingers.

"Twenty-one, twenty-two, twenty-three..." She counted out loud, her brows pulled together with concentration.

She looked towards her mom who approached her and grinned widely. "Mom, my period came on the same date again."

My eyes widened in realisation. I just missed my period. It was supposed to come on the week before this.

Could it be?

I walked out of the washroom in a hurry to speak to Declan when I collided into a wall.

"Sorry." I muttered under my breath, looking up to see Mr. Anderson.

I cursed under my breath for not looking in front of me and knocked into him. Otherwise, I wouldn't have to bear looking at him.

"Hi, Mr. Anderson." I greeted with a forced smile, hating the fact that we were alone right now.

No one knows what he would do to me.

"Hey, gorgeous." He winked in an attempt to flirt as he picked up my hand and kissed my knuckles.

I almost threw up.

I yanked my hand away, wiping off his saliva with the material of my dress.

"That was gentlemanly. But Declan will not like that, so please refrain from doing that again." I stated, smiling awkwardly at him.

"Declan? Does he let you call him by his name or are you his girlfriend?"

I was totally stunned by the question thrown in my way. Girlfriend? Are we even an item?

"You must have misunderstood. We are purely just boss and secretary." I tried to explain even though he looked unconvinced.

"So, is that why he has been protecting you everytime I tried to get you under my skin? Are you sure about that?" He taunted, taking a step forward as he pinned me against the wall.

"Mr. Anderson!" I screamed, struggling against him as the tearing sounds of my dress filled my ears.

My dress was now torn to my chest where my bra was visibly showing. My legs were shaking as hot tears rolled down my cheeks.

"Hush, baby. I will make this less painful for you." He reassured, grinding against me as he tried to remove my bra.

He was suddenly ripped off from my body, making me sigh in relief as I closed my eyes.

I was saved.

++++

Vote. Comment. Share

Enjoying this book? Add this book to your library and your reading list.

22nd November 2016

24: Unknown Savior

A punch was thrown his way, cracking of knuckles instantly filled the empty walkway.

I tried to pull up the remaining of my dress, covering as much as I can. My teeth clenched tightly as he was continuously being beaten up by my unknown savior.

His back was faced me so I couldn't see properly who it was.

Finally with one last blow, Mr. Anderson was completely knocked out while the man slowly rose.

He turned around, eyes meeting mine as he raked his eyes across my appearance.

My legs trembled with fear as I shivered under his gaze, praying that he was not going to prey on a victim like me.

I had enough of all these bullshit.

He took big steps to approach me while I ended up moving towards the wall until I was cornered with nowhere to run.

I closed my eyes, not exactly anticipating what's to come. I only hoped that someone will help me.

I was suddenly pulled into something warm as a thick material draped across my arms.

Slowly, I peeled my eyes open to see him buttoning up the blazer as his eyes met mine.

"Better?" He asked, tucking strands of hair behind my ears.

I gulped, bobbing my head up and down since I didn't know what to say at this moment.

"I will laundry it and return to you as soon as possible." I whispered, shivering slightly from the light breeze as it sent shivers down my spine.

I was about to leave when he stopped me abruptly. As if on autopilot, I raised a brow in response.

"Hold on, how are you going to return the blazer to me?"

My lips formed an 'o' in realisation. "You can leave your contact on my phone." I said, picking up my phone as I handed it to him.

He simply smiled, showing dimples which made him look kind of cute.

As he entered the buttons, I heard noises from around the corner. Curiously, I took a few steps forward and turned around the corner to see two figures making out in the shadows.

Her skirt swayed as she grinded against the guy who looked so familiar from this distance away.

The guy, however, pushed her away and stepped out of the shadows.

It was Declan, that f*cking bastard.

And he was making out with Mr. Anderson's PA. That b*tchy sl*t.

Fuming in rage, I turned to leave only to see my savior ushering me towards the direction of exit.

I forced a tight smile, walking beside him as we walked down the walkway.

"Babe!" The all too familiar voice chased after me as I felt a tug on my arm. I was turned around and pulled into his arms as his eyes met mine.

"Please hear out my explanation, babe. It's not what you think it is."

I pushed him away with a grunt in frustration. "Shut up, I don't want to hear anything from you." From my baby's father.

My hand rested on my abdomen as I turned around and walked out of the place with my savior who kept silent this whole time.

I felt betrayed, again and again. How many chances was I supposed to give him before it all ran out?

I shouldn't have let him have the chance to hurt me again.

Before I knew it, tears rushed down my cheeks as I sobbed like a lost soul. It was uncontrollable, tears just flowed down with no sense of direction.

An arm was wrapped around my waist as he pulled me into his arms. I stood there, letting him comfort me in this peaceful silence.

++++

He pulled up by the curb, stopping right in front of the lobby. I wiped away my tears, looking towards him with a forced smile.

"Thank you for the ride." I whispered, already losing the will to speak anymore.

"Do you need me to accompany you?" He offered, smiling down at me with the dimples which could have swooned many women at the sight.

However, I was the least interested since I was going through a rough patch right now.

"It's fine, I can be on my own." I said, climbing out of the car as I slammed the door shut.

I walked up the steps just as the door was opened. "Call or text me if you need a listening ear." A husky voice belonging to him erupted from the back as I turned around and smiled, trying not to let it affect me so badly.

"Okay, I will." I replied back, moving towards the direction of the door as tears continued to flow freely.

++++

Vote. Comment. Share

Enjoying this book? Add this book to your library and your reading list.

3rd December 2016

25: A Surprise Visit

The moment I reached the house, the first thing I did was to drop to my knees. Silent cries filled the living room as I broke down instantly.

I can't take it anymore. At this point of time, I felt like dying.

I have a life in me. Yet, I was backstabbed again and again by the baby's father.

Why must my life turn out to be this way?

All hopes were lost. That once strong and confident woman was gone. All that was left was the little fire burning in me.

Yet, it was slowly extinguishing by itself, leaving me torn and broken.

I just don't know what to do with my life anymore.

++++

I was planning to stay in my house for the entire day, just sleep and eat until it becomes a routine.

Since I have applied for all of the leaves I have not been using for the current year, I might as well use up all of them completely before I tender my resignation.

Working under him was a mission made impossible. It kills me to even see him flirting with another woman who isn't me.

What's more? He even went against his promise and cheated on me. This jerk doesn't even deserve to be a part of my baby's life.

He can rot in hell for all I care.

I touched my abdomen with my hand tenderly as I smiled. I had done a pregnancy test and it showed two red lines.

It was positive.

The day after tomorrow, I was going to have a checkup at the clinic to confirm.

All will be good.

Knocks pounded on the door rapidly as I tensed, wondering if it could be boss.

I sighed, climbing out of the bed as I slowly walked towards the door.

I peeped through the small hole and instantly sighed in relief when it was the unknown savior who saved me.

In fact, the name shown was Terence when he saved his number in my contacts.

I opened the door, noticing a broad smile on his lips.

"Morning sleeping beauty, have I woke you up?" He greeted with a certain cheerfulness in his tone.

I laughed, "Not really, I was going to climb out of bed anyways."

"Then I am glad I am here with breakfast." He said, lifting the plastic bag in his hands.

I raised a brow in response. "That's surprising. Come in."

He chuckled huskily. "Trust me, there will be a lot more surprises coming from me."

"Well, I'm looking forward." I shrugged casually, moving towards the kitchen as I set up the blender.

It has been so long since I had surprises. I have a feeling that I was going to enjoy his presence from now on.

"What are you making?" He asked, quirking an eyebrow in curiosity as he leaned against the island counter casually.

"Apple juice." I replied, not looking at him. When I was about to get the mugs, I looked up, noticing him staring at me intently.

Was there something on my face?

"Why are you looking at me like that?" I asked, raising a brow.

He merely chuckled in response. "You look beautiful even when you are focusing on the blender."

I was dumbfounded by his words. He was literally so straightforward with his words when we barely knew each other.

"I will take that as a compliment." That was all I managed to choke out as I quickly turned back to whatever I was doing.

Another deep chuckle came from him while I focused on making the apple juice.

A song was played on the radio and I began moving my hips to the beat. It was a calm and relaxing song that I don't mind dancing to it all day.

The apple juice was finally done and I poured it into two mugs.

I turned around to see him staring at me until his eyes landed on the mugs I was holding.

"Thanks." He took it from me and began drinking while I moved towards the couch silently.

Sitting down on the couch, I turned on the television as the news anchor appeared on the screen.

"It has been reported that Mr. Anderson was attacked by an unknown man and was found unconscious on the ground by his PA."

There was a picture of him laying unconscious on the ground with his face badly bruised.

I turned towards Terence who was staring at the screen without any emotions. His eyes met mine as he smiled. "He deserved it anyways."

I shook my head. "You could have been implicated if you were caught. I can't watch you going to jail because of someone like me."

"Someone like you? I will never blame you even if I land in jail, Natalie. I will do anything for you."

Wait, how did he know my name when I didn't even give him my contact number?

I shot up from my seat, staring at him. "Who are you? How the hell did you know my name?"

++++

Vote. Comment. Share

Enjoying this book? Add this book to your library and your reading list.

9th December 2016

26: Childhood Sweetheart?

I leapt out of the couch and stared at him warily, literally switching to a defensive mode.

If he tried to do anything to me, the umbrella stand just by the door will be aimed on his head.

"Don't worry, I am not here to harm you. If I wanted to do that, I would have strike first." He reassured with a tight smile.

For some reason, I believed his words and calmed down slightly.

"Have you forgotten me, Natalie?" He asked while I stared at him without a clue.

"Who are you exactly?"

He chuckled huskily, quickly covering his disappointment as he smiled. "Still remember the little boy who used to piggyback you around whenever you were injured or bullied?"

Flashback

I felt myself being pushed to the ground, hitting the big rock next to me. I cried at the sight of blood.

The big bad bullies were laughing at me, saying how weak I was. I continued to cry until a boy much older than me chased them away.

He came up to me and pulled me up while I continued to cry. He bent down to a duck position and made me go on top of him.

I did and he carried me like this for the rest of the day as we had fun in the fields.

I felt that I was no longer alone again.

I smiled at the memory, realising that the little boy was actually him.

"You are him?" I confirmed again, my eyes twinkling brightly with hope.

He smiled. "I have always been here for you." He widened his arms and I rushed forward and hugged him.

He carried me up and spun me around. By the time he placed me down, I was feeling nauseous again.

I quickly rushed to the bathroom and threw up all my lunch.

It felt so horrible to be pregnant.

A hand patted on my back warmly as he comforted me in silence.

"Are you not feeling well, Natalie? Shall I get some medication for you?" He offered while I raised a hand to stop him.

I wiped my mouth clean and stared straight ahead. "There's no need for that, I am just pregnant."

"Pregnant?"

I sighed, shaking my head at the state I was in. Even when I am pregnant, I am still going to go through this alone.

"Who is the baby's father?" He asked, making my heart numb upon mentioning him.

I ignored his words and washed my hands instead to keep myself busy.

When I rose to look at the mirror in front of me, his eyes stared straight into mine with coldness in them.

"Is it... him?"

My eyes widened as I turned around to face him. I dropped to my knees and grabbed onto his hands.

"Please don't tell him. I don't want him to know that I have his baby." I cried.

He pulled me up and held onto me tightly. "Why would I even let a bastard like him know that he has a baby? He doesn't even deserve to be a part of the baby's life."

I held onto him as if he was my lifeline and cried my heart out. My heart was hurting so badly, it was tearing apart.

I hated the fact that he could make me fall in love with him and he could make the pain so unbearable.

I hate myself for allowing him to hurt me.

++++

Vote. Comment. Share

Enjoying this book? Add this book to your library and your reading list.

18th December 2016

27: Pregnancy

After that day, he never mentioned about the baby's father again. Instead, he was caring and understanding towards me.

I walked alongside him as we walked down the streets where road stalls were set up.

Somehow, he managed to entwine his fingers with mine halfway through the walk.

I was fine with that since it gave me a sense of nostalgia. I missed holding onto him like how we usually did in the past.

Ever since he moved to another place, we never got into contact again. Surprisingly after so many years, we reunited again.

This time in a more awkward situation though. But nevertheless, it was still great to catch up with him.

It distracted me from a lot of things which were not worth mentioning. This was what I needed right now, especially when I was pregnant.

Tomorrow would be the day where I will check to confirm my pregnancy.

I was determined to protect this baby at all costs, away from the man who hurt me so badly. Even if it meant tearing the father and child apart.

The smell of fried chicken made my stomach growl in hunger. My eyes focused on the fried chicken wings as I licked my lips in anticipation.

Without a word, Terence pulled me along with him as he sat me down by a table. "Stay put, I will get some chicken wings for you."

My heart instantly warmed at how caring he was. He was so different from him.

What have I done to deserve this second chance? Perhaps, I could forget the past and start afresh with this man in my life

++++

Entwining my fingers together, I felt sweat all over my palms. I was praying hard that the baby I was carrying was real.

"Don't worry, everything will be fine." Terence assured as he kissed my temple while massaging my shoulders as it calmed my nerves slightly.

I looked at him, trying my best to smile as I bobbed my head up and down in response.

Dr. Carter flipped through the pages of the results while my heart beat dramatically faster than before.

It was so nerve-wrecking.

She smiled, her eyes twinkling brightly. "Congratulations, you're 5 weeks pregnant."

My eyes lit up in joy as I can't help but to smile. His hands held mine as he kissed my temple. I looked at him, feeling nostalgic when he was by my side.

I shook off the thoughts, knowing that at this point of time, I shouldn't be thinking about him at all.

"Babe, are you okay?" Blinking profusely, I thought I saw him in him again as I closed my eyes tightly.

I was hopeless.

"I am just tired, I need some rest." I replied, opening my eyes once more as his eyes met mine.

He smiled, supporting me as he led me out of the office after thanking Dr. Carter.

The whole ride home was pure silence. Guilt was eating on me each time I tried to look at Terence.

Perhaps it was going to be hard putting him behind me. I just need some time alone for now.

As he pulled up by the curb, he began to unfasten his seat belt. He reached over and unfastened mine.

My eyes caught sight of him lingering behind a car as his eyes were on us. Impulsively, I pulled Terence towards me and kissed him.

I wrapped my arms around his neck and continued to kiss him with no care for the world.

F*ck him, I don't want to care about him anymore. I need an escape from him.

My eyes opened once more to see him banging on the window repeatedly.

His veins popped out as he clenched his jaws tightly. If looks could kill, we would have been ten feet under.

He was in a rage.

++++

Vote. Comment. Share

Enjoying this book? Add this book to your library and your reading list.

24th December 2016

28: A Fight

He ripped open the door and pulled Terence out of the car. A blow was sent his way as he beat the crap out of him.

My eyes widened incredibly. I pushed past the door and tried to break them apart. "Stop!" I yelled which earned a slight push from him as I stumbled backwards.

I held onto my belly protectively and glared at him with hatred.

Terence punched him in the guts and kicked him as he fell backwards.

Terence flew to my rescue and gently caressed my cheeks. "Are you okay?" He asked.

I nodded, still holding onto my belly protectively.

"Babe?" His sickening voice made me rush to the drain as I puked.

A hand tenderly stroke my back as I took in a deep breath. I turned around to see Terence supporting me while I slowly stood up.

"Get your bloody hands off my woman." He growled, pushing away Terence as he pulled me into his arms.

I tensed.

Tears that has been withheld for so long finally released as I cried my heart out. "Let me go, Declan."

"Babe?"

"I'm not your girlfriend anymore, you have no more rights to call me that. Let me go."

"Even when we haven't dated, you still allowed me to call you that." He reasoned.

I pulled away from his arms and slapped him.

"That was when you were shamelessly flirting with me when we were working. But none of that matters anymore because I have decided to quit."

Hurt flickered across his eyes as he stared at me, astonished. "What?"

I looked away from him, knowing that I would fall under his spell again if I continued to look at those bewitching eyes.

"You heard me loud and clear, Declan. I am breaking up with you and quitting from this job. Go find another woman to screw." I spat with hatred as I walked towards Terence and fell into his arms weakly.

He managed to catch me and carried me in bridal style as he entered the lobby.

"Don't worry, it's over." He cooed, kissing my temple as he entered the lift with me in his arms.

I closed my eyes, letting my tears continue to spill as I embraced the moment in silence.

Things would never be the same again.

++++

He handed me a mug of hot chocolate, sitting down beside me in silence. I stared at the mug absentmindedly.

"Care to talk?" He asked, brushing his thumb across my eye bags as he wiped off my tears.

I placed the mug on the table and turned to face him. "That guy was both my boyfriend and my boss. Turns out years ago, he was the one who took away my virginity."

I could feel his body tense as he remained silent. I took it as a cue to continue.

"He kept silent about it from the day I stepped into his office until the day he got his hands on my heart and got into my pants once more."

For some odd reason, my heart pained more than anything else as tears spilled down my cheeks uncontrollably.

He shifted towards me and wrapped his arms around my waist. I leaned my head against his chest and heaved a huge sigh.

"I don't believe in love anymore, Terence. I don't want to have my heart torn again."

++++

Vote. Comment. Share

Enjoying this book? Add this book to your library and your reading list.

31st December 2016

29: Unable To Resist

It felt so much better having the troubles lifted off my chest as I confided Terence last night.

It was as though no one but him truly understood how I felt.

That was enough for me.

The lift 'dinged', signaling that I have reached my destination as the doors opened.

I took in a deep breath and stepped forward as I entered the place where I used to work.

Like I have said, I was quitting this job. Even if he got till his knees to beg me, I will never waver.

The fear of him knowing that I was carrying his baby was still there. I feared that he would fight for the custody of the baby and take my baby away from me.

No way in hell will I allow that to happen. The last thing I wanted was for my baby to follow in his footsteps.

I mustered my courage as I stared at the door in front of me. My hand wrapped itself around the door knob tightly as I opened the door.

F*ck this shit, I'm not going to care about him anymore. He doesn't deserve my attention.

The first thing I saw was a zombie version of him seated on the desk as his eyes were closed.

Eye bags were visible, his hair was in a mess as though he had tugged on it several times.

Everything about him, even his shirt dress was untucked with creases.

I can't believe how much he had changed in such a short span of time.

Was he going through what I was currently going through as well? Or was it all an act just to fool me?

Get a grip of yourself, Natalie. You have to be strong for the unborn baby inside of you.

I cleared my throat, noticing a grunt coming from him as he massaged his temple.

"Didn't I say that I don't want to be disturbed?" He groaned in annoyance.

"It's me."

This instantly got his attention as his eyes peeled open. Joy flickered across his eyes as he stared at me.

"Sorry," He paused, quickly adjusting his suit as he slowly made his way towards me. "I didn't know it was you, babe."

I frowned deeply. "Don't call me that anymore, Declan. Like I have said, we are already over."

It was as though he was burned by my words, his joy turned into sadness quickly as he continued to stare at me.

"Please don't do this to me, babe. Let's talk." He offered, trying his hardest to change my mind.

This only made me think of him as a pathetic jerk. He should move on, instead of trying to make me stay.

"It's no use trying to change anything, Declan. I have already made up my mind." I calmly stated, wishing for a million times that my hormones was not acting up at this timing.

It was making me so incredibly horny, unable to resist those lips of his.

F*ck, this pregnancy was making things worse. I should flee when I have a chance.

"So what if you have made up your mind? I am not going to let you go this easily." With that said, he pulled me into his arms and kissed me with no care for the world.

Unable to resist him, I felt myself reacting to the kiss as I deepened it.

F*ck, I have certainly lost it.

Our lips molded, moving in sync as he pulled my body even closer towards him. My arms found his neck, wrapping them around his nape tightly as I pulled him in for more.

I missed this feeling of our bodies close to each other. If only things hasn't turned that way, we would still be together.

The door suddenly flung open, startling us as I broke away from the kiss.

I turned around to see Terence staring at us in shock before it quickly turned to anger.

++++

Vote. Comment. Share

Enjoying this book? Add this book to your library and your reading list.

Apologies for the short chapter but I'm already trying my best to lengthen it! No promises, but I will try to update at least twice a week ;)

7th January 2017

30: Regret

"**T**erence..." I trailed off, not knowing what to say as he caught us molding lips together.

F*ck, if only I could have controlled myself, maybe things wouldn't have messed up.

His eyes were burning through my skull as he clenched his teeth tightly.

"I thought you were different from other women, Natalie." He spat angrily. "Perhaps, I was wrong about you."

I slowly walked towards him, shaking my head. "I'm sorry, Terence. I-I didn't want things to turn this way either."

He took in a deep breath and looked at me closely. "Admit it, Natalie. You have been taking me for granted while you were pregnant and alone."

A tear rolled down my cheek as I digested his words. What he has said was a fact, I was just a selfish bitch who couldn't get over the man who broke my heart so badly.

"And, your heart did not stay with me either." With that said, he turned and left.

I stood there, stoned. All I felt was guilt and remorse at this moment.

He was right, I had taken his feelings for granted.

Declan suddenly turned me around and stared into my eyes. "Babe, you are pregnant?"

I didn't know what happened, but the next thing I know, I was hitting him.

"It's all your fault, asshole. It's all your fault for landing me pregnant. It's all your fault for not ending your playboy ways. It's all your fault for breaking my heart once more." I cried, feeling his arms encircle my waist tightly.

Eventually, I stopped fighting and let my sobs fill the whole room.

"I'm so tired of everything." I whispered, leaning against him with heavy eyelids.

++++

I woke up, finding myself at a deserted place. I looked around me to find nothing but trees.

My eyes found a pair of eyes staring back at me. A beautiful little girl with two pigtails.

She widened her arms and smiled widely, revealing her dimples. "Mommy."

I carried her up and spun her around in delight. She giggled, laughing at the same time as we went in circles and circles.

"Tania..."

I jolted awake as I noticed Declan hovering over me with concern.

"Are you alright, babe?"

I stared at him, confused. "What happened?"

"You kept calling out Tania's name in your dream. Did you encounter a nightmare?"

I shook my head, slowly turning to the side as I held onto my belly protectively. The baby might be a girl.

If the baby is really a girl, I will name her, 'Tania'. She will not take after her father's surname, but mine instead.

I have decided to raise the child by myself.

"Babe? Are you still mad at me?"

I rolled my eyes. "I don't see a need to respond to you. Get out."

He sighed, slowly shutting the door before he left.

I closed my eyes, letting hot tears fall freely as I can't let my child grow up normally like the rest.

I won't let my child acknowledge the father. I don't need him in my life anyway.

31: A Broken Trust

A hand gently trailed along my skin, moving from my jaws to my cheekbones.

I knew who it was, deciding to act like I was asleep just to chase him off.

"I know you're awake, babe." His raspy voice rang in my ears as his thumb caressed my lips.

Sighing, I peeked my eyes open and stared at the man in front of me.

"What do you want?" I grumbled, not in the mood to talk to him, much less breathe in the same air as him.

"I know you're angry, babe. I know you can never forgive me but please, give me a chance to clear the misunderstanding between us." He whispered, hope flickering across his eyes.

I raised a brow and heaved a huge sigh. "Does it matter anymore?"

He clasped onto my hands tightly, staring into my eyes solemnly. "It does, babe. You know that I love you more than anyone else. Why would I screw Mr. Anderson's PA when I already have you?" He explained.

"So what? You expect me to believe what you have just said when I saw it with my own eyes that you were swapping saliva with her?" I snapped gruffly.

"Don't you trust me?" He whispered softly, looking into my eyes with disappointment.

"Changing the subject doesn't help, Declan. You might as well admit how good she was in bed." I spat angrily, rage growing with every seconds.

"I have enough of your lies, Declan. I am never going to trust you again."

With that said, I stood up and attempted to make a move forward when pain took over.

I held onto my belly protectively, suddenly feeling afraid that something was going to happen to my baby.

He stared down at me frantically as concern was written all over his face. "What's going on, babe? What's happening to you?"

Those words were the last thing I heard from him before darkness took over.

++++

Beeping sounds surrounded me as I groaned, stirring from my sleep.

My back ached at the rough texture of the mattress, wishing that it was smooth instead.

Perhaps, my sleep would be prolonged.

I peeled my eyelids open, the first thing I saw was Declan resting his temple against the bed as he slept soundly.

I shifted to the side slightly, moving my hands to trace the features of his face.

I was so engrossed in tracing those lips of his when his hand abruptly caught mine.

I gasped, finding his eyes meet mine. He wrapped his arms around my waist and nestled his head in the crook of my neck.

"Have anyone told you how shameless you are just to make a woman return to your side?" I grumbled like a cranky woman.

"Not when that woman is carrying my baby. I will never let this woman go, no matter what happens."

"You're sick, you know that?" I spat in anger, covering my belly protectively.

"Keep in mind that I will never let this baby acknowledge you as the father."

He sighed. "Babe, I know I don't deserve your trust now. But, I want you to know that I will never stop loving you."

"You can say that when you are on your deathbed, Declan. For now, just get out of the ward otherwise, I will get myself discharged and move back home."

32: In A Heartbeat

I looked away, frustrated with this guy as he persistently tried to get my attention. "Please, babe. Give me a chance to explain myself. I swear that I loved you and no one else. I will risk my life to protect you."

"Protect me?" I questioned scornfully in disbelief.

Lies. His mouth were always full of lies and nothing else. I will never believe this man again.

"If you have not been busy kissing his PA, perhaps you would have saved me from being raped by that man!" I screamed with hate and disgust dripping from my voice.

"Even thinking about it makes me sick to the core." I whispered, tears spilling down my cheeks with horror as memories of what happened that night flashed across my mind.

"What?" He stared at me, jaws clenched tightly in anger. "How did he..." He trailed off, only to be suddenly reminded of something.

"It all makes sense now."

I stared at him with confusion and disbelief. "What the hell are you talking about?"

He sat down next to me and caressed my cheek, leaning his forehead against mine. "I'm sorry. If only I hadn't drunk that spiked cider, I wouldn't have mistaken her as you."

I tensed. Was he speaking the truth?

"Things wouldn't have turned this way." He whispered, his voice full of remorse and guilt.

I stared at him, my heart softening as it hurts to see him like this. It wasn't his fault. It was those two who broke us apart.

Eventually, it was also my fault for not placing my trust on him.

"It isn't your fault." I wheezed out after a moment of tensed silence. "It's the trust between us that was easily broken."

He snapped his eyes up at me, staring at me intensely.

"You know what?" I sighed heavily, a mild headache already forming. "I just want to sleep and get this over with."

"Babe..."

"I want to start afresh with you." I said with determination, closing my eyes briefly.

A kiss was placed on my forehead as I looked up to see his loving eyes staring into mine.

"You're willing to forget about the past and forgive me, I can't be any happier than this day."

His eyes rested on my belly, staring at his child lovingly. I smiled, taking his hand as I rested it on the surface.

"Feel the heartbeat? It's ours." I softly said, admiring the look of awe in his eyes as he stared at our product of love.

"I can't believe that I am going to be a father soon either." He chuckled, pulling me in for a kiss.

I melted into his arms instantly, wrapping my arms around his neck as I longed to have those lips of his on mine.

Passion ignited in our souls and we made love again, this time, his focus were on me.

Only me, and no one else.

I wouldn't have it any other way.

Epilogue

M onths later...

Putting down the bowl of congee, I licked my lips happily as my cravings were satisfied.

A tissue gently wiped away the remaining rice stuck to my lips as he smiled down at me. "Look at you, babe. I think I would never grow tired of watching you growing so plump each day."

I looked up at him with a frown settling on my face. "What are you trying to say? I'm fat?" I hissed, crossing my arms in anger.

Oh god. Ever since the pregnancy, my mood was constantly swaying. I have no idea how to control my temperament during this period, making me so frustrated at times.

He began to panic. "You know this isn't what I am trying to say, babe. Even if you wear extra size, I will still love you like before."

Instantly, as though a child was given a candy, my anger began to diminish upon his words.

I groaned aloud. "Why are you always so good with your words?"

"Isn't it the reason why I always seem to get you on bed?" He teased jokingly, pulling me onto his laps.

I wrapped my arms around his neck and let out a soft purr. "Really? I thought you were taking advantage of my hormonal sex cravings?" I retorted back with a smug smirk.

He grunted out loud in response. "As much as I tell myself not to touch you while you are still pregnant with our baby, I can't seem to keep my hands off you."

"I know you are just trying to make me feel better since I am getting so plump now." I sighed in despair, not liking the fact that as my bump was growing every day, my body size was also growing as well.

By the time I have given birth, all I get are fats and excess skin. Why is the process of having a baby so difficult than I thought it would be?

"Babe, look at me." He gripped my chin gently to face him. "Even if you grow more plump, I will still love you."

"I-" My words were cut off, my face scrunching up as a wave of pain hit me.

"Babe?" He shook my shoulders, looking at me with concern. I leaned into his touch, holding onto my belly protectively.

"The baby..." I trailed off, sweat trailing down my forehead.

"The baby? The doctor said our baby will be due next week." He whispered to himself as he began to panic upon noticing my state.

It wasn't until the water bag broke did my eyes widened. "The water bag broke. The baby..."

Without needing to be asked, he hurriedy carried me in his arms as he rushed out of the house in a hurry.

++++

"Push!" The doctor urged, making me push as hard as I could. My whole face turned red out of breath as the torment continued.

"I see the head already. Push!" I screamed out loud at the immense pain, clutching onto the sheets tightly.

As each second passed, I felt even more lethargic. I lost my voice and energy after exerting all my strength.

Eventually, I gave it all in and heard the sound of baby crying filling my ears.

I panted heavily, staring at the little figure craddled in the doctor's arms as he continued to cry.

"Congratulations, it's a baby boy." The doctor smiled.

I heaved a huge sigh in relief until I suddenly felt a wave of pain hitting me. I screamed out loud at the pain as I shifted uncomfortably on the bed.

"She is losing a lot of blood. We need a blood transfusion immediately." The doctor rushed out her words as the nurses began rushing in and out of the labor room.

I felt darkness embracing me as I allowed it to take over. The last thing that was on my mind was the relief that my baby is safe and sound.

That's all that matters.

++++

A buff figure appeared in front of me as I stared straight ahead. He turned around, smiling down at me.

"Dad?" My eyes shimmering with tears as I stared into the familiar brown orbs.

He was standing a few feet away from me as a small portal appeared out of nowhere. I approached him, my smiles getting wider until the frown settled on his face stopped me.

"Dad?" I asked again, stopping in my tracks as I continued to stare at him.

"Are you happy?" He asked. I smiled, remembering of my husband waiting for me and my baby son who has just born into the world.

I looked up to see him shaking his head. I raised a brow, confused. "Dad?"

The next moment, he was waving me away from him, away from where he was going.

He smiled lovingly at me, tears running down his cheeks as he turned to leave. I gasped, watching helplessly as he entered the portal which slowly disappeared into thin air.

I felt my knees touching the ground as my tears flowed freely. I finally understood what he meant.

I was given a choice to either follow him and join him or stay put and bring myself back to life.

Eventually, my smile revealed my answer. And without needing to ask any further questions, he has already given me his blessings.

"Thank you, dad."

I looked up at the sky, feeling the strong wind brushing across me. "My darling, always be happy." A voice carried itself along with the wind before it was gone.

I felt myself awakening in my body once more as I tried my hardest to slowly reign control.

I moved my fingers, hoping for some form of reaction.

"Babe? Are you able to hear me?" A familiar voice entered my ears as I perked up in delight.

It seemed like I was slowly gaining control. I pushed myself to exert more strength as I peeled my eyes open.

Light flashed across my eyes as I gasped, slowly adjusting to the light. A blurry figure rested in front of my eyes, my focus slowly getting clearer.

Declan stood in front of me, his eyes red and puffy from crying. He rushed to my side and caressed my cheek. "I am going to get the doctor, babe."

He was about to run off when I held onto him tightly. "I-" My throat was clawing at me for water as I looked towards the jug beside me.

He seemed to have understood what I wanted as he quickly poured me a glass of water.

Supporting me to sit up straight, he let the rim of the glass touch my lips as he helped me.

I gulped down the water hungrily. All the screaming and lack of water has made me so thirsty.

He placed the glass back down, sitting on the empty spot beside my bed.

He caressed my cheek, looking down at me with concern. "Are you alright now? I will get the doctor to check on you."

He was about to leave once more when I grunted in frustration. "I don't want to see the doctor, I want to see my baby."

He chuckled huskily, quickly nodding his head as he rushed out of the room.

I conjoined my hands, wanting nothing more but to see my baby boy right now.

When he arrived with the baby, I was surprised to see his beautiful orbs staring up at me as he smiled.

I cooed, craddling him in my arms as I rocked him. My eyes took noticed of his sharp nose to his large eyes, copying his daddy so much.

"My baby boy." He snuggled into my embrace, closing his eyes once more as he fell fast asleep.

"Just by seeing him safe and sound, all these effort is worth it."

"But seeing you almost dying, I felt my whole world crumble before me." He whispered, tilting my chin to face him.

He encircled his arms around mine, burying his head on the crook of my neck. "You don't know how my world instantly crashed the moment the nurse announced that you're losing a lot of blood and you needed a blood transfusion."

"I am sorry." I whispered apologetically, wishing that none of these had happened.

He looked up, staring into my eyes intently. "I lost you once to Terence," He paused, holding onto my hand tightly. "I lost you the second time to Hades."

"But I am never going to lose you again."

2nd February 2017

www.ingramcontent.com/pod-product-compliance
Lightning Source LLC
Chambersburg PA
CBHW070403200726
48294CB00003B/1070